Duffle Bag Cartel 2

Lock Down Publications and Ca$h Presents

Duffle Bag Cartel 2
A Novel by *Ghost*

Duffle Bag Cartel 2

Lock Down Publications
P.O. Box 870494
Mesquite, Tx 75187

Visit our website @
www.lockdownpublications.com

Copyright 2019 Duffle Bag Cartel 2

Lock Down Publications
**Like our page on Facebook: Lock Down Publica-
tions @**
www.facebook.com/lockdownpublications.ldp
Cover design and layout by: **Dynasty Cover Me**
Book interior design by: **Shawn Walker**
Edited by: **Tammy Jernigan**

Stay Connected with Us!

Text **LOCKDOWN** to 22828 to stay up-to-date with new releases, sneak peaks, contests and more…

Thank you.

Submission Guideline.

Submit the first three chapters of your completed manuscript to ldpsubmissions@gmail.com, subject line: Your book's title. The manuscript must be in a .doc file and sent as an attachment. Document should be in Times New Roman, double spaced and in size 12 font. Also, provide your synopsis and full contact information. If sending multiple submissions, they must each be in a separate email.

Have a story but no way to send it electronically? You can still submit to LDP/Ca$h Presents. Send in the first three chapters, written or typed, of your completed manuscript to:

LDP: Submissions Dept
Po Box 870494
Mesquite, Tx 75187

DO NOT send original manuscript. Must be a duplicate.

Provide your synopsis and a cover letter containing your full contact information.

Thanks for considering LDP and Ca$h Presents.

Ghost

Chapter 1

That night I held Shanté in my arms as she shook. Her teeth chattered. I'd been holding her for a full two hours, and there had still been no change. We were at Kamya's house, and I was doing all that I could to calm my baby down.

Kamya came out of the kitchen with a apron wrapped around her waist. "'Dinner's ready y'all, its time to put some food in your stomachs." The aroma coming from the kitchen smelled amazing. Like fried chicken, macaroni and cheese, cornbread, and pound cake. Kamya might have only been eighteen years old, but she was a southern woman already. Her cooking skills were second to none.

I loosened my hold on Shanté so I could stand up. She grabbed even tighter. "Daddy. No. No. Somebody's going to try and kill you. Please don't go. Please daddy."

I felt so defeated. I kissed her cheeks. "Baby I'm not going anywhere. We're both going to go in here and eat dinner. You don't have anything to worry about."

She shook her head. "I'm not hungry, but I don't want you to leave me."

Man I'd never seen my daughter so afraid before. It was the most demoralizing feeling in all of the world. I wanted to break down and cry, and at the same time I wanted to murk a million people that had ever hurt a child before.

I sat Shanté on my lap, and fed her a little bit of food off of my plate. She ate it reluctantly. After we had our fill, she took a bath, and I held her until she fell asleep. Stroking her cheek, and kissing her forehead every few minutes. I loved my daughter with everything I had inside of me.

After I put her to bed, I jumped in the shower and washed the day's poison off of me. I didn't know what I was going to do, or how I was going to handle things with Mikey. I didn't know if I should come clean to him about Alicia and I, or if I should just see how he would play things down the road. I knew that this option would be the most dangerous. Mikey was a loose cannon. He had the ability to snap out about things out of the blue. That's what I wanted to avoid. Him snapping out could have meant death for me, Alicia, Shanté, or my unborn child. I just had no way of knowing. On the other hand, maybe coming to him like a man would soften the blow that was sure to come. I didn't fear Mikey. No, not at all. He was my homeboy. Had he been any other nigga, I would have knocked his head off and kept it moving. Life was too short to live in paranoia. I didn't like worrying about anybody doing something to me. I felt that the easiest way to avoid paranoia of a enemy was to get rid of them by any means necessary. Mikey got the benefit of the doubt because he was like my brother, as cliché as that may have seemed.

At the conclusion of my shower, Kamya came into the bathroom and dried my body from head to toe, while I stood in front of her naked. "Phoenix you should feel lucky that you and my lil cousin are alive. I don't know what the fuck is going on, but I can't stand to lose you. I love you so fuckin much." She dropped the towel, and kissed my lips hard, while hugging my body to hers. "Damn."

I slowly wrapped my arms around her body, and rested my lips on her forehead. That was a habit of mine. "That's why I gotta kill them niggas, shawty. I been ducking these fuck boys for way too long. I tried my best to let Mikey run the show because he had all of the plugs. Dat shit over wit now though. I'm finna run shit. I'm finna get rid of these Black Haven niggas, then me and Mikey need to sit down and get an understanding. We can't get rich with him running shit, or there being bad blood between us. Somethin gotta shake."

Kamya lowered her head. "Is it true that Alicia's carrying your baby?" She whispered.

I shrugged my shoulders. "It might be, I mean we have fucked around a lot, and the dates add up. If it is, I ain't got no choice other than to do the right thing."

Kamya smacked her lips. She pushed me off of her. "Damn Phoenix. I can see you fucking her a few times, but pregnant? Man what the fuck? I ain't enough for you or something?" She turned her back to me.

I pinched the bridge of my nose, exhaled and slid behind her pulling her back to my body. "Kamya, me and her was fuckin around way before you and I was. Besides all that, you're my blood, shawty. You know can't shit good come from what we're doing. Pretty soon it has to come to an end."

"An end?" She turned around and faced me. "What the fuck are you talking about Phoenix? I love you. I gotta be with you. This ain't no you and Sabrina type of shit. This is my whole ass heart we're talking about. You can't just sever things when you're ready to. That's not fair cuz. I'm a long way from being able to do that." She slid her arms on to my shoulders, and laid her head on my chest. "Do you love me?"

I nodded. "Yeah Kamya, I love you. You're my baby."

"N'all, Phoenix. I'm not talking that family love shit. I mean do you honestly love and care for me as a man would a woman?" She looked into my eyes. "The truth baby, because I'm crazy about you. I don't care how silly I may sound. do you really love me?"

I brushed her pretty hair out of her face, and fixed it so that it stayed behind her ears. "Yeah Kamya, I love you as a woman. You are my baby, and there is nothin in this world that I wouldn't do for you, shawty. You should already know that."

She smiled. "I do."

"Kamya but we can not be together in that way that you want to because you we my cou--." I started.

She pressed her finger to my lips. "Ssh, this is Memphis, Phoenix. Damn near every household down here is doing what we're doing. You're just over thinking things. Just trace our family's history." Kamya took her finger away from my lips and sucked it into her mouth. "I need you right now. I need you to lay me down, and to fuck me good. My lil pussy getting wet from just thanking about it right now. Huh feel." She slid my fingers into her panties, and rubbed them over her bald pussy lips. They were meaty and hot. My middle finger slid into her tight hole. Her lips wrapped around it "Unnnn, yes." She placed her foot on top of the tub.

I added a second digit and got to fingering her pussy her wet pussy at full speed. I sucked on her neck, and cupped her perfect titties through her white t shirt. Her nipples were stiff as erasers. I sucked them one at a time.

"Yes. Yes. Phoenix. Yes. Gimme some cuz. Gimme some of that dick, you got me so horny fo yo ass." She dropped down, wrapped her fist around my stalk, and stroked it up and down, while putting the head into her mouth, and sucking on it hard. Deep throating me as far as she could take it. Gagging along the way.

I pulled her up. "Bend yo ass over that toilet. Come on."

Kamya stuck her ass into the air, and held on to the back of the toilet. 'Fuck me cuz. Put all that dick inside of me, please." She begged sucking on her bottom lip.

I ran the big head in between her lips, and pushed it home. Slid all the way in. She arched her back and moaned. I rubbed all over that fat ass before going to work, long stroking her at full speed. Her ass crashed into my lap, jiggling and shaking. That pussy was hot as lava, and soft as cotton.

"Uh! Phoenix. Yes. Yes. Fuck me. Harder. Harder. Aw fuck!"

I closed my eyes and kept on pounding while holding her little hips. I was trying to hit her bottom. I felt a draft on my ankles. The door creaked, causing me to open my eyes. Before I could react, it was too late. I felt cold steel pressed to the back of my neck.

Kamya continued to moan loudly, unaware of the intruder.

"You bitch ass nigga, I can't believe you. You gon do this to me." He pressed the gun harder into the back of my head. "You gon fuck my wife, and get her pregnant. This is the last piece of pussy you gon ever get!" Mikey growled, causing Kamya to scream at the top of her lungs.

"Shut up Kamya before I lace yo ass too, wit yo trifling ass. Fuckin this nigga. Ugh." He pressed the gun harder into the back of my head. "Explain yourself nigga."

I clenched my jaw and slowly allowed my piece to slide out of Kamya. "Let my cousin up out of here. She ain't got shit to do wit this. Me and you can handle this shit like men." I could still feel the wetness from Kamya's pussy on my dick. Her scent was loud and heavy in the small bathroom. While I worried what Mikey's next move would be in regards to myself and Kamya, I feared for the safety of my daughter e. She was sleeping peacefully in the next room, oblivious to what was taking place in Kamya's bathroom.

Mikey wrapped his arm around my neck. "Nigga you ain't running shit. You should have thought about her wellbeing when you got to doing this snake shit behind my back. Grab that bitch cuz."

Korky, Mikey's cousin, came into the bathroom and snatched Kamya up by her hair. "You coming wit me bitch! Lets go." He proceeded to drag her out if the bathroom.

I tensed up, angry. I saw the way he was handling my cousin and it pissed me off. I wanted to murder him and Korky. Kamya had nothing to do with our beef. This nigga was taking being petty to another level.

Kamya kicked her legs wildly. She struggled against Korky. "Let me go. Let me go, muthafucka. I don't even know you!" She screamed, as he pulled her all the way into the front of the house.

Mikey took me and threw me forward. I stumbled and caught my balance. We wound up in the kitchen. He kept his gun trained on me. "Why Phoenix? Why would you betray me like that? Why fuck my bitch?" He asked with his lip curled.

I mugged him for a long time in silence. "Mane, me and shawty was fuckin way before y'all even thought about getting married. Ain't nothing personal. Once y'all tied the knot we ceased and desisted that shit. You taking this shit way too far nigga. At the end of the day pussy is pussy, and that's all it is. Ain't no such thang in niggas like us marrying no bitch. We been playas from the beginning."

"Don't kick that bullshit to me, Phoenix. What you did was some fuck shit. You betrayed me my nigga. You fucked the only woman I've ever loved behind my back, got her pregnant, then plotted with her on how y'all was gon leave me in the lurches. Yousa bitch nigga in every sense of the word." He cocked the hammer.

I could hear Kamya fighting with Korky somewhere in the front of the house. I was praying that Shanté didn't wake up. I felt that as long as she was sleep she would be safe.

I inhaled and held my hands at shoulder level. "So what, you gon kill me? Over this shit? That's your game plan?"

He shook his head. "Nigga if I killed you it would be over and done with. You wouldn't experience half the pain that I need you to. So n'all, I ain't gon kill you. I'ma make yo bitch

12

ass suffer. First, I'ma do this." Mikey aimed and fired. *Boom. Boom.*

One bullet slammed into my shoulder, knocking me backward. I felt the stinging pain immediately. I flew into the wall. The second one knocked a chunk out of my thigh. It hobbled me. I fell to the ground. "Ahh. Ahh. Muthafucka." I clenched my teeth again. Sweat was pouring down the side of my face. I mugged that nigga , and lowered my eyes. I could feel the blood leaking out of my shoulder.

"That's what the fuck you get Phoenix. Nigga you lucky I don't kill you right now. Lucky. The only reason I'm not is because I can use yo punk ass. I'ma ride you all the way to the top. No homo." Mikey kicked me in the chest, and knocked me backward, placing his Jordan on my neck.

He was treating me like a straight bitch. The pain was excruciating. My vision went hazy. All I could think about was my daughter, Shanté. As long as he took things out on me, there should be no reason for him to hurt her. I had to take what I was receiving for fucking around with Alicia. Karma was a bitch, and she had her heels on my throat right now.

"You see that bitch, Nastia is obsessed with your ass because of Taurus, and the blood y'all share. That's the only reason I ain't fuckin you all the way up right now homeboy. That bitch represents a whole lot of money, power, and prestige. I gotta have all of that shit. It's time that a real nigga like me reigns supreme."

More blood leaked out of me. I was shaking and I felt cold. The pain intensified. "Nigga, you done popped me over a bitch. I can't believe this shit. Now what?" I pushed his shoe off of my chest, and scooted back on my ass until my back rested against the refrigerator. My teeth were chattering.

"What now?" He laughed. "Now you earn your daughter back nigga."

My heart sank.

"I'ma use you to finesse this Nastia bitch. Once I get in where I need to be, I'ma take over her whole outfit. Then you can have your daughter back, and move on wit your life. I ain't want shit to be this way Phoenix. You fucked me in the game first. You did this."

As if on cue, two of the Brooklyn niggas came from the back of the house with Shanté. Her wrists, ankles, and mouth were duct taped. I could her screaming into the tape. Tears fell down her caramel cheeks.

I struggled to get up. "Gimme my muthafuckin daughter you bitch ass niggas!"

Mikey kicked me in the ribs, knocking me to the floor. "I'll be in touch nigga. Go get yourself cleaned up. Nastia got a move she want us to bust in a few days." He walked away laughing.

I struggled to use the refrigerator to stand up. Blood rushed out of my thigh, and my shoulder. "Mikey! Mikey! Don't do this to me, Mikey. That's my baby!" I hollered. "Mikey! Come on man!"

Kamya rushed into the kitchen after they left the house. I heard their tires peel away from the curb, and I knew they were gone. When she saw me she broke into a fit of tears, and fell beside me. "Oh my God, Phoenix. Oh my God." She looked me over and saw all of the blood.

I fell to my back, and began to shake so bad that I couldn't think straight. I was in so much pain, both in my heart and my body. Not only had Mikey popped me twice, but he'd taken my daughter. *Shit had gotten really real* were my last thoughts before my eyes rolled into the back of my head.

Chapter 2

I owe my survival to my cousin Sabrina. Somehow, someway, Kamya had secretly gotten me over to her clinic. Once I was there she worked tirelessly to get me right. Between getting the slugs out of me, hooking me up to an IV, and a blood transfusion, Sabrina said it took her three days. I couldn't remember of anything, just a lot of pain. Every time I opened my eyes it felt like she was poking or prodding me with something new. I felt freezing cold, and my mind would only travel back to Shanté. I couldn't believe that I was in a fucked up position. That I'd screwed things up so much that my daughter had been taken in the cross fire. What was a man if he couldn't protect his child? I was miserable. beyond sick. So after the initial three days of my surgery, it took another four before I felt strong enough to open my eyes.

When I opened them on the seventh day, Smoke, one of my young hustlers from Orange Mound was standing over me with four of his lil homies standing behind him. "Say Mane, Sabrina told us what that fuck nigga Mikey did. That shit ain't cool, Potna. Whad'ya you say we holler at that fool, and them East Coast niggas on some rest in peace shit? Every since he came back from visiting New York he been low key shitting on us country boys. He got dem niggas making mo' money den us. They already riding foreign whips and thangs, when the home front ain't even got one car yet. That ain't how that shit supposed to go. Dis been Memphis way before he brought them New York niggas into the equation. You been one hunnit since the beginning, Phoenix. That's more then I can say for him." Smoke lifted his shirt. His entire waistline was filled with multiple hand guns. "Nigga we ready to murder some shit for you right now, homeboy." He looked over his shoulder toward his crew. "Dat Duffle Bag shit you was hollering bout.

15

Nigga we bout all dat." All of his crew lifted their shirts. They had just as many handguns as he did.

I struggled to sit back on my pillow as I took the oxygen feeder out of my nose, inhaled a deep breath and swallowed. My throat felt drier than a desert. I tried to clear it and smacked my lips. A sharp pain shot up through my shoulder. I wanted to scream like a bitch. "I appreciate you lil niggas, Mane. Real talk." Swallowing slowly , Itried to gather myself.

Smoke handed me the juice box off of the table, and held the straw to my lips. "Try some of dis shit right here Mane. Yo throat sound kinda raspy."

I took it out of his hand, and downed the juice. It felt cool going down my dry throat. I tried to clear it again with better success. Coughing, I set the juice box on the tray on the side of the bed. "He took my daughter lil homies. That nigga playin the game on a whole other level." I winced in pain as I adjusted myself on the bed once again. "Y'all fuck wit me and on everythang I love, I'll help all of us to become rich in less than a year. I got a plug out of his world, Mane. All that Rebirth flow is because of me. Now believe that shit, like a true story."

Smoke nodded. "Playboy that's what we here for. Mafuckas already know where the grass is greener. I'm saying right now that me and my niggas are choosing you. Mikey done already chose his New York kinfolks anyway. So what's the move? I say we bring that heat to that nigga tonight, or as soon as you can get up out of that bed. On some real shit, you ain't even gotta be there. We'll go sweat that nigga on our own just to let you know that we riding wit you. You got us eating. That nigga ain't on shit. As long as he feeding them Brooklyn niggas he taking food out of our mouths. Our families starving and shit. If that pussy put a slug in his right hand man, he'll do all types of worse shit to us, so fuck that." He pulled his nose. "We'll hit that nigga right now. Its yo call homie."

I shook my head. "He got my daughter man. Anything go wrong and he could put that steel to her. Nall, I gotta use my head. We gon fuck this nigga over, but we gotta do it at the right time. Let me sit down wit this fool first. Pick his brain, and find out what he on. As soon as I discover or detect any weakness, or where my daughter is, we striking. I wanna murder this bitch nigga in a sadistic fashion. I'm talking on some shit that's gon turn the city upside down."

Smoke nodded. "Hell yeah. That's what we talking about." He looked back and shook his head at his crew then turned back to me. "Aiight Homie, gon do your thang. We'll wait in the weeds. However, in the mean time we tryna get our scratch right. You da the plug that got the plug. So we tryna eat wit you. The Mound is jumping. We did that shit. That's our homeland. We got them pigs Links and Jack on deck. Everythang is running smoothly. We wanna venture out a lil more. Sew the whole area up wit that Rebirth shit. All we need is for you to sign us up under you. We'll kick the Duffle Bag shit off right now. Make me and the homies official."

I felt a sharp pain resonate in my thigh. It felt like I was being stabbed in the thigh with a steak knife over and over again. "Look fellas, why don't y'all let me holler at the homie Smoke for a second so we can get some thangs understood."

Smoke nodded. "Yeah, say Mane, y'all step into the hallway real fast. Let me see what the big homie talking about."

His crew grumbled, and one by one came over and bumped fists with me before they stepped out of the room. They wished me get well soons, and all other kinds of good tidings. We waited until the door closed behind the last person before we resumed.

"Phoenix, I already know after fuckin wit a nigga like Mikey that its gon be hard for you to trust anybody. I ain't got no problem proving myself, and my loyalty to you. When its all said and done I just wanna feed my kids, man. I'm down to die for the nigga whose helping me to feed them. You already know how the game go. I heard that you was fuckin Alicia and all that. Even though it ain't right, that shit ain't nothing to hit a nigga up over. He was supposed to check his bitch, not his nigga. Bros before pussy holes, you feel me?"

I didn't know what to say behind that. I knew I was bogus. Real niggas didn't behave in the fashion that I had. Mikey was supposed to be my dawg. Fuckin his wife was out of order, but I didn't have no dick control, that's just me being honest. "Enough about me and Mikey's relationship. I'll deal wit that shit later. I wanna holler at you when it comes to this Duffle Bag shit." I fluffed my pillow and fixed it behind my back, then sat up as straight as I could. My lungs felt like I was inhaling ice for some reason. "I wanna fuck wit you lil homie. I wanna make you my right hand, and allow you to man yo lil niggas in the Mound, and outside ofthe bitch. I want us to get rich, while at the same time I work on getting my daughter back. What you thank about that?"

"I'm wit it. Like I said before, shit already rolling in the projects. We got feens coming all the way from Black Haven to cop our Rebirth. Long as we keep a steady supply we should be rich in no time. But,what about Mikey? You already know he finna try break some shit up. That nigga got your daughter, Mane. Long as he got that kind of collateral he can do anything to the mob and ain't nothin that we can do about it. That's why we gotta nip that shit in the bud right away. At the same time we gotta drive on Dragon and his Black Haven crew. Them niggas touched a million plus when they hit Mikey the first time. They used that shit to cop them fully automatics from the Asians on the east side. Man they been spraying shit down every since. That fool Dragon is a problem. Right now its a struggle for the streets. We gotta make our foot prints known. This the wrong time to be beefing inside the clique."

"I agree lil homie. There are a lot of moves to be made, and its on me to lead us in the right direction. I'm finna turn up over my daughter nigga. Believe that shit. I got Mikey. But for now, I need y'all to fall back and let me twerk this connect. You about to see more money than you've ever seen. Trust me on this. Get yo niggas ready for that trigger shit too. Expected the unexpected. From this moment on its me and you nigga. I got this." I held out my hand.

He shook it. "I'ma be that nigga for you, Potna. Let's get this money, and let's shut this city down. Memphis belongs to us. We ready to move however you say, when you're ready. Until then I got a half of brick of Rebirth left. That's fifty gees in product. Me and my niggas gon rock that shit until its gone."

***

Fourteen hours later, after I came out of a deep sleep, I woke up to find Kamya standing on my right side. Her hand on my chest hand was resting on my chest and her eyes were red. "I thought he killed you Phoenix. I thought he took you away from me. If he had I don't know what I would have done. I love you so much." She leaned in and kissed my lips softly. Then with more force Sucking on the bottom one.

Sabrina opened the door and came into the room just as Kamya was breaking our kiss. She stopped and placed her hand on her waist. "Ain't this a bitch. I should of known that yo fast ass was gonna be sniffing around our cousin, Kamya.

You try and do everythang that you see me do." She snapped, walking closer to my bed side.

Kamya waved her off. "Dis ain't got nothin to do wit you Sabrina. Get over yourself. I been crushing on Phoenix since the beginning. Me seeing y'all fuck a few times only pushed me over the edge. But it ain't about that right now. Its about him getting better, and me being by his side while he does." She rubbed the side of my face.

"Well all dats cool and what not, but I'm sorry cuz, you gotta to go before my supervisor call the police. She let you stay this long with out reporting it as a favor to me. She's reached beyond the limitations of what she was supposed to allow. If they find out that we brought in a patient that was suffering from gun shot wounds, and we didn't report it to the local authorities, both if us could lose our credentials, and catch a hefty fine. So you have until morning. You hear me?" She kissed my cheek.

"That's cool. I feel a lil better anyway. I knew I couldn't stay here too long."

Sabrina rubbed my chest. "I'm sorry about Shanté. I hope she's okay. I know for her and Toya to be missing the way that they are has to eventually take a toll on you.

My daughter's mother had been missing every since Dragon and his boys attempted to assassinate me a few months ago. I didn't know if she was alive, or dead. While me and Toya weren't in a relationship, I still cared about her because she was the mother of my daughter. My entire beef with Dragon came from the murder of his cousin Bryon after he put his hands on Toya. Every since then it had been nothin but war and chaos.

"I appreciate that, but its all good. I'm figuring shit out. Far as Kamya goes." I grabbed Kamya by the waist, and pulled her closer to me. Allowed my left hand to roam all over her thick ass cheeks. "This my lil baby right here. Shawty the only one that can keep me sane."

Kamya smiled, and laid her head on my chest. "I wish you didn't have to go through this Phoenix. Its not fair. I wish I could do something to help you." She hugged me tighter.

Sabrina looked on jealously. "Get yourself together Phoenix. You gotta be fine by the morning." She kissed my cheek, and left out of the room.

As soon as she disappeared, Kamya wiped Sabrina's kiss from my cheek. "I don't like her kissing all on you and stuff. Dang. You need to tell her that that ain't cool. I mean unless you want me too cause I ain't got no problem wit it."

I laughed. "Calm yo lil jealous ass down. You looking too far into shit. Get yo lil ass up here and lay on me until I can figure out my next move." I ordered.

She smacked her lips, and straddled my waist, after kicking her shoes off. Her skirt rose on her hips. The scent of her perfume got stronger. She rested her face within the crux of my neck, kissed it, and sucked on the hot skin there. "Anyway you need me Phoenix I'ma hold you down. I don't give a fuck about us being cousins. I'ma be yo gansta bitch from here on out because I'm crazy about you and I don't want no bitch taking my place under no circumstances. Every real nigga need a ride a die bitch sitting to his right and that's me. You need to teach me how to wet up some shit, and I'll bust my gun for you on a regular basis. You got my word on that baby." Her small hand caressed the side of my face. She pressed her lip to my cheek. Kamya had always been the real affectionate type. Even before I hit that pussy.

Once again I took a hold of that fat ass by sliding her skirt upward. I cupped them cheeks. "Lil cuz I'm about to turn into a nigga that you don't wanna see. This man that you see right now is about to cease to exist. I'm finna turn all the way up."

"And?" She kissed my lips. "Whatever you do, I'm finna do. I'm not leaving your side. If they kill you, they gon have to kill me. That's just that." She slid down in the bed and popped my dick out of my shorts, took a hold of it in her fist, and began to pump it, looking into my eyes with her light brown ones. "You think whatever you're about to become is going to scare me? Phoenix, man, you got another thing coming. I'm bout all that lil daddy. Long as I'm yo ride a die bitch, I'm bout all that." She sucked me into her hot mouth, and her head became a blur as it moved back and forth in my lap giving me immense pleasure.

My eyes rolled into the back of my head. I tightened my fingers in her naturally curly hair. Laid back, and put my plan of action into motion inside of my mind. With my daughter's life on the line there was no way that I could afford to lose.

Chapter 3

"Aiight nigga, when we go in front of this bitch you just act like everythang is normal. She about to cut us in on somethin that's gon get us right. I don't need you fuckin that up. You got me homeboy?" Mikey asked, stubbing his Newport out in the ashtray of the Waldorf Astoria hotel we were waiting inside of.

I mugged him from where I sat on the couch across from him. I could still feel the pain from the bullets that he'd put inside if my body. I couldn't wait to pay his bitch ass back. Even though he had the upper hand because he had my daughter somewhere hostage, that didn't mean that I was going to allow him to treat me like a bitch. I had too much heart for that. "Say Potna, you can quit all that tough talk. You ain't threatening shit over here nigga. I know how to handle this bitch. If its one thing I'm good at its finessing a ho." I smiled at his weak ass, and grabbed the bottle of the champagne from the table that had been set out for us. "Besides, whatever we got going on ain't got nothing to do wit shawty. That's two separate thangs." I popped two Percocets, and downed them with the champagne. My wounds were killing me. "How is my baby Mane? You taking good care of her?"

Mikey crushed up his Percocets and made two thin lines on the table, then tooted one of them. He pulled on his nose, then pinched his nostrils together. "She good nigga. I ain't looking to hurt that baby. She still my God daughter. Dis ain't about me hurting her, unless I have too, its more about me hurting you. You been on some real fuck shit."

I clenched my jaw and mugged this nigga as he tooted another one of the lines, and tossed his head backward. I had a mind to pull out my Forty Five and pop him twice through the neck. I would knock big chunks out if his shit, leavehim bleeding, and stomp his face to death. I hated the sight of him. I imagined how he interacted with my daughter, and it made me sick to my stomach. I wondered who bathed her? If he fed her on time? I wondered about what he fed her? Was she eating? How did she sleeping? Did she cry all the time? How did he handle her when she did cry? There were so many questions going through my head that it was making me dizzy. Instead of saying another word to him I turned the bottle all the way up and waited to feel the Percocets kicking in. I needed the numb feeling. I was tired of the pain.

Mikey picked his head up. "Another thang Phoenix. You gon start hitting my hand every week with no less than fifty gees nigga. I'm expecting to get paid from you every Friday come hell or high water. Nigga just to keep me from putting a bullet in yo head, that's what it's gon cost." He laughed at that.

I stood up and flipped the table. "Bitch ass nigga, what's happening? I ain't paying you shit. Fuck I look like?" I pulled the gun from under my shirt and cocked that bitch.

He didn't even look up at me. "Nigga sit yo punk ass down. The last thing I'm worried about is you pulling that trigger. You do that and the lil homies already got word to crush your daughter, after they make a woman out of her lil ass." He looked up at me, and frowned.

I aimed the gun at him. "Fuck you just say nigga?" I cocked the hammer, ready to splatter his tomato.

He scoffed. "Nigga you heard what the fuck I said. You don't put that gun down and yo shawty gone get it in the raw. I don't give a fuck how old she is, this is war nigga. Now sit yo Bitch ass down, or pull the trigger fuck you waiting on?" He snapped, lowering his eyes.

I swear to Jehovah man, it took everything in me to not blast this fuck nigga. Now he had all types of bogus images going through my mind. I began to worry about exactly what they were doing to my baby girl. I saw that I couldn't really trust him to keep his filthy hands off of her, or his crew's hands off of her. This bitch nigga was sicker than a person with pneumonia.

The handle to the door shook. I took my seat on the couch. Then it beeped, and the next thing I knew Nastia was walking into the hotel room being escorted by two big, beefy security guards. "Boys. Boys. How have you been?" She asked, looking more tanned then usual. Her long, blond hair fell past her waist. She allowed for her leather Burberry jacket to be removed from her.

Mikey stood up, and took her hands in his. "I can't speak for nobody else, but I'm doing good as can be. Getting my money right just like I thought I would once I linked up wit you, Queen." He kissed her on both cheeks.

She smiled and looked over her shoulder at me. "And are you the only one that is happy to see me?"

I frowned and looked away. I wasn't in the mood to be polite. I was missing my daughter like crazy, and worrying about her safety and well being. Nastia in that moment didn't mean shit to me. I didn't care that she had all of the best dope in the city. I didn't care that she was plugged in ways that most kingpins could only imagine. The fact that she had rolled real tough with my uncle Taurus back in the day, and because of him, and the sharing of our bloodline, she'd become obsessed with me, meant nothing to me in that moment. All I could think about was Shanté. My baby girl.

"Phoenix, did I do somethin wrong to you. Are you angry wit me?" She asked, releasing her hands from Mikey's.

"You ain't did shit to me. I just got some thangs on my mind that's all." I said, picking a piece of lint off of my pants and flicking it onto the floor.

"Aw Nastia, the homeboy just having a lil family problems. You know how it is." Mikey offered. He looked nervous, and must've felt that I was going to mess things up. I was sure that he was accustomed to how bad my temper was. When I got into the kind of mood that I was in now I didn't give a fuck about nothing. I wanted to murder his ass. In my mind's eye, I could see him laying on the pavement twisted, with a puddle of blood under him.

Nastia shot an angry glance to him. "I don't need you to speak for him Mikey. Why don't you have yourself another drink. Wipe some of that powder off of your nose." She took out a handkerchief and tossed it to him.

caught it, and sat down mumbling under his breath. He wiped his nose clean, and mugged me with mounting hatred. Once again I saw myself smoking his ass. As soon I figured out where my daughter was, his ass was grass. That was a guarantee.

Nastia extended her hand. "Phoenix, I need to speak with you in the other room. Now, please. Come on." She leaned down and slid her hand into mine. Hers felt soft, and smelled of some expensive perfume that I couldn't finger.

I got up and followed her into he back of the hotel room. Once there, she walked up to me and kissed my lips, licking all over them. "What's the matter baby? Did I do something wrong? If so tell me what I did?" She found my gun, tossed it on the bed unbuttoned my pants, and slid her hand into my boxers. Nastia took my dick out, sniffing the head into her right nostril. "Mmm, you smell so good. I love the scent of this big black dick." She licked along the length of it until it hardened. Slowly pulling the shoulder straps to her dress off of her shoulders, Nastia allowed her big breasts to spill out. Her melons bounced briefly as they freed themselves. The pink areolas covered the majority of her tits. She rubbed my

26

dick all over the nipples. "Talk to me baby. What can I do to make you happy?"

I grabbed a handful of her blond extensions, and yanked her head backward. "Bitch I ain't say nothin was wrong wit me. Maybe I'm not feeling yo as right now. You ever think of that?" I growled. I didn't give a fuck how much power this bitch had. She was still a snow bunny to me, and I had yet to fall in love with, or to feel some type of way about a white girl. That just hadn't happened, and I didn't think it ever could. Besides this bitch used to fuck wit my uncle Taurus. Not only was she way older than me, but I just wasn't feeling her like that. All she was to me was money.

She shuddered. "Uh! I love the way you talk to me Phoenix. Talk that shit to me then. Do it."

I pulled harder on her hair and made her yelp. "Bitch suck this young, black dick. You know that's all you care about."

Nastia groaned louder and sucked me into her mouth. She was slurping me loudly adding plenty of spit, moaning, and groaning loudly. Her hand pumped me at the same time. "Tell me baby. Tell me I'm your bitch. Tell me this white pussy belongs to you. Tell me what I can do to make you happy?" She moaned, popping me in and out of her mouth.

I spaced my feet, and got to fucking her face like it was a shot of pussy. Although I wasn't in that mental sexual space, I couldn't deny her head game. It was amazing hot, wet, and tight. The scent of her was too much. Her moves were on point like she'd been sucking dick every since she was a shawty. When her teeth nipped at the head of my piece, I shuddered. My toes curled, and then I was cumming in her mouth, blasting like it was a shoot out.

Nastia gripped my dick harder, and pumped it up and down, swallowing my baby makers. Her lips were pursed tight around my head, greedy for more of my release. When she had swallowed all that I could muster, Nastia stood up and pulled her skirt all the way up her hips. "You already know what I need baby. I need you to put that black dick right between these. Seductively she ran her finger in between her bald lips, and sawed it up and down. She was wetter than a puddle of water.

I picked her lil ass up and threw her in the bed roughly, grabbed her by the throat, and licked her face. My dick rubbed along her inner thigh. "Bitch you don't call no shots with me. I run this shit. You got that?"

She arched her back and opened her legs wide before sliding her hand between them, and dipping a finger into her wet hole. The digit shot in and out of her at full speed. Her thighs tensed. "Yes. Yes baby. Un, please fuck me."

I flipped her over. "Get on them knees bitch. Let me spank that ass. Let me get that ass red hot before I fuck you from the back. Right in this mafucka right here." I opened her ass cheeks, and ran my finger in a circle around her anus. I was so irritated that the only thing I could think about was mistreating her ass. I was about to bust that back door all the way open. I wanted to put his bitch in her place once and for all. Then it would be time to talk business. I was sure that my uncle used to handle her the same way. I couldn't confirm it, but I just felt like doing the most with this bitch every time she was in my presence. That had to be my blood taking over me, It was in my DNA.

Nastia got to her knees and tooted her ass up into the air. Her face laid sideways on the mattress, looking back at me. "Go ahead baby, smack them. Smack them hard. Treat me like a white whore."

And that's just what I did. I started smacking that ass hard. I'd raise my hand high in the air, and bring it down as hard as I could. She'd yelp, and ball the sheets into her fingers toot her ass higher, just so I could beat it some more. After the fiftieth lick Nastia went crazy. Her pussy was oozing , running down her thigh. "Fuck me Phoenix. Fuck me. Put that black cock in my pussy. Please. I swear I'll do whatever you want. Just do it."

I got behind her, and stuffed my shit into her. My nails dug into her hips and I got to fucking her as hard as I could with long strokes. Her pussy was hot and tight. Her ass hole winked at me with each plunge. I smacked them cheeks, and pulled her long hair roughly.

"Aw, yes! Yes Phoenix. Fuck this pussy. Fuck this pussy. Harder. Harder. Harder. Uh. Uh. Uh. Uh. Yes. Yes. Yes. Aw. Aw. Aw. Aw. Fuck me. Fuck me." Nastia crashed back into me over and over, encouraging me to go harder. Her pussy oozed like crazy. She kept getting wetter and wetter.

I was growling like a angry lion, killing that shit from the back. Nastia's big breasts jiggled back and forth, slapping against her stomach as she endured my assaults. I couldn't help but watch my black dick going in and out of her pink lips. It was fascinating to me.

"Phoenix. Phoenix. I'm. Gonna. Cum. Baby. Your black dick. Aww. Your black dick is.... Awwww! Yessssss!" She screamed.

I slapped that ass and forced her on her stomach, plunging as hard as I could. Nastia shook underneath me, and begged me to go harder and harder. My piece was like a piston going in and out of her. Suddenly, I was pulling out and cumming all over her ass cheeks and lower back. She sat up and sucked me into her mouth, wiped her juices off of me and smacked her lips. "Damn Phoenix. Jesus Christ. I'm going to need to take you on a trip wit me. Maybe for a week or so. I need you to do some things to my body that I'm too shy to say. She licked all over the head again, and sucked her way up my stomach. "How does that sound baby?"

"That depends on how much money you're about to help me make before then."

Chapter 4

Nastia sashayed into the room, and dropped two duffle bags on the floor in front of me. She knelt down, and unzipped one of them. "Look, this is a hundred bricks of the Rebirth. Fifty in each bag. I am placing them at your feet to show you how serious I am about your advancement in that game out there. I wish you would simply come and be a kept man for me. I would make it so that you never have to worry about anything. We would take trips to foreign places. I would buy you whatever you want, line your pockets with as much cash as you want and you would never have to do anything other then fuck me long and hard. I wish you would commit to this but something tells me that it's not even an option."

"Its not. Now tell me what you want in exchange for all of this merchandise? I knelt beside her and took one brick out of the bag at a time. They felt heavy. They were wrapped in aluminum foiled packages with yellow smiley faces all over them. I didn't know what the smiley faces represented, and I didn't care. The Rebirth was a money maker. If I wanted to I could take each brick and step on it with some lactose. I could add eighteen zips to each kilo, and the Rebirth would still be powerful enough to keel the feens knocking down our doors like bill collectors. These bags represented money, and power. Power that I would need to annihilate Mikey, and Dragon's bitch ass.

"I have to go away on business for fourteen days. While I am away I need to ask you a personal favor?" She kissed my cheek, and rubbed my back.

I continued to count the bricks, praying that she wasn't on no fuck shit.

"Yeah, and what's that?" I asked.

"I want you come with me baby, so that while I'm talking with the big wigs you can keep Natalia company and safe. She's always complaining that all I leave around her is grumpy old security guards. I'm tired of hearing the nagging. I need you to watch over her, and to pull a move for me while we're out in Moscow. A personal favor. You chill with me for two weeks and all of this is yours. Of course you'll have to cut Mikey into the equation some way. He's already agreed to make the trip with us. But that's still open for discussion." She kissed me on the side of my mouth.

I really didn't like this Bitch kissing all over me and shit, but like I said before she was a cash cow. She represented prestige to me. I needed to keep her closer than the words in a sentence. The closer she remained to me, the faster myself and my cartel would move up the ladder. Once I got my daughter back, I had plans on making a few million, and getting out of the game. I was gon settle in one if those islands that didn't have extradition, and call shots to my cartel from there. Every so often I would make a pit stop in America. That would only be to look over my operations. For me, Memphis, was just a start. I wanted to control the whole south. I wanted to be rich, and great. Put that shit that my uncle Taurus did back in the day to shame.

"I don't need that nigga looking over my shoulder. I can handle this assignment on my own. On the flip side I ain't no fucking baby sister. Why you can't get one of them out of shape niggas to watch over Natalia?" I zipped the bag, and started to count the bricks in the other one.

Nastia, stood up. "I could provide my child with the best security team in the world, but I choose to put you on the job. After all she is your cousin. I'm pretty sure that you would protect her more than either of them ever would. Plus you guys are the same age. You'll have more in common with her then anyone of my team. Besides, a hundred kilos Phoenix... That's quite the pay out and you know it." She licked her thin lips. "So what so you say?"

I stood up with both straps to the bags in my hands. "How many of these bricks do I gotta give to Mikey?" I knew that the more shit I gave him, the richer he became. He was already asking me to drop fifty gees a week as a payout. Since I was already giving Links and Jack ten a piece that meant that I was about to shovel out seventy thousand every Friday. I had to hurry up and put a end to Mikey's calendar like the Mayans. That bitch ass nigga.

She shrugged her shoulders. "That's up to you. But that is your boy right? Although I am detecting a bit of animosity between the two of you. Is there something going on that I don't know about? If so, tell me so I can fix it. I don't like seeing you like this. There is a lot of tension in the air even between us and I've been nothin but good to you every since I found out that you were Taurus's blood."

I began to stuff one duffle bag as much as I could. I left ten bricks in the other bag and kept ninety for myself. My bag looked deformed but I didn't care. "Shawty it's good. Me and the homie just going through some thangs. We'll figure it out. We always do. Anyway, I'm giving him ten bricks. I'm keeping ninety for myself, and my crew. I'm looking to be a King all by myself. I don't need Mikey or no other nigga. From here on out you're funding me and I'll see to it that he get what he get. You understand that." I stood up and pulled her to me roughly, slid my fingers into the tresses of her hair and made a fist, pulling at the roots.

"Ouch. Yes baby. I hear you. I heard you loud and clear." Nastia's nipples began to telescope through her Burberry blouse. Her face flushed. She looked like she was in heat all over again.

I looked into her steel blue eyes, for a long time. "You want you a young black killa don't you?"

She shivered. "What?"

I pulled on her hair harder. "Don't play wit me, bitch. You're obsessed with this black and white shit ain't you?" I led her all the way back and slammed her against the wall of the hotel room, hard. I pressed my forehead to hers. "Answer me bitch."

She started breathing hard. "Why do you talk to me like that? It drives me crazy."

I grabbed her neck, and squeezed, choking her just a bit. I just wanted to see how she was going to react. Slowly, I applied pressure. Her face turned a burgundy like red, before I let her go.

She let out a gust of air, and continued to breath heavily. Then she attacked me. "Fuck me right now Phoenix." She reached for my belt, and tried to release it. "Please fuck me right now Phoenix!"

I threw her back against the wall, holding her by her wrists. "Calm your ass down and be smooth. Its a time and a place for all of that. For now I gotta go and get by people right. I'ma take you up on that two week offer, and its cool, Mikey can come along too. I'm pretty sure we'll find some way to put him to good use. Just remember what I said to you. I'm looking to be my own king. I don't need no other nigga riding my coat tail. Especially since this shit should be all about me and you." I stroked her hair, then rubbed the side if her face. It was time that I played on her emotions. Since she was acting all obsessed with me and shit, I felt that was in my best interest to play into that. It would make things a whole lot easier for me. Even though she looked about fifteen years older then me, and clearly not my type at all, the bitch was a boss and that was all that mattered.

She froze, and looked into my eyes as if she was trying to search my soul. "What are you saying Phoenix? Are you saying that you're not opposed to giving you and I a try?"

I shook my head, and thought to myself that this broad must if been out of her mind. She was making shit way too easy for me. I didn't understand how a woman could have come into so much power, and at the same time be so emotionally gullible. I didn't think that was possible. I stroked her cheek. "Nastia, I got a whole lot of work to do before I can step into any relationships but when I'm ready you'll be the first to know." I kissed her lips, and hugged her to my body.

She allowed for me to hold her for a few moments. then she took a step back and gazed into my eyes again. "Phoenix, the worst thing you could ever do is to play with my heart. There are only two things in this world that are sacred to me, the first is my daughter. The second is my heart. If either one of these particular things are hurt in any way, I can not be responsible for what happens to the person that did it. Do you understand this?" She pushed me away from her, and walked away to look out the big window that over looked the water. "I'm falling for you Phoenix. I don't know how I am, but I am. I'm falling for you, real hard, and its scaring me."

***

On the drive home I slid the duffle bag over to Mikey, who was sitting in the driver's seat of his fresh Range Rover Sport. He was parked in front of Kamya's crib, with Meek Mill's Championships banging out of his speakers. "Huh nigga, here go ten more brick of that Rebirth. You should be able to get right off of this." I'd told Nastia where to drop the other duffle bag with the additional ninety off, first thing in the morning and she'd agreed. I couldn't risk Mikey's bitch ass asking me what was inside of the other duffle bag. He still had by daughter, so everything he asked me for until I had her back, I would have to grant. I hated that fact with all of my cold heart.

"Now dis what the fuck I'm talking about, Playboy. Dis shit ain't got nothing to do wit that first fifty bands you owe me though, right?"

I cringed. Man, this nigga was getting on my nerves. "Say Mane, we got an understanding. You ain't gotta keep bringing dis fuck shit up, Potna. I'ma have that lil scratch for you. Now let me see my daughter, Mane, what fair is fair."

"Nigga get yo pussy ass out my truck fuck nigga. You sitting there talking that cowboy shit. Muthafucka, I ain't showing or letting you talk to no muthafucka until you put that bag in my hand the first time. You better get it through yo head, you ain't running shit homeboy. All you are is a muthafuckin pawn. As soon as I see that you're of no more use to me yousa dead man. Pow. Pow. Pussy nigga. You gon feel them slugs Mane. Betta pray yo baby don't feel em too." He curled his lip. "Get the fuck out my shit. Gon. Get!" He hollered as loud as he could.

I sat here with my head lowered and my trigger finger itching. I wanted to murder this chump. I wanted to put five in his face but I had to keep Shanté at the forefront of my mind. A nigga had to remember that I was my baby's only line of defense. If I fucked up and made the wrong decision, I could cost my daughter her life. With that on my mind, I pulled on the lever and let myself out of his truck.

"Yeah bitch nigga, have my money, or find pieces of that lil girl all over the city. You created this war, nigga. Now I'm her daddy." He reached over and pulled his door closed, just as I upped my pistol from my hip, ready to blow at his punk ass. Mikey stepped in the gas laughing like a true fuck nigga.

I watched his truck until it disappeared from the block, and turned the corner. Minutes later I walked into Kamya's crib dejectedly. She was sitting on the couch reading a book called *A Bronx Tale* by Ghost. She saw me and set the book on the table. "Hey Phoenix. I was just thinking about you."

I don't know where they came from, but all of the sudden tears began spilling out of my eyes. My heart felt as if it we're being ripped in two. I was so angry that I felt like killing a whole community of people. I missed my daughter, and I needed to see her to make sure that she was okay.

Kamya was about to make her way over to me, but when she saw the waterworks she stopped. "Cuz what's the matter? What the matter, please talk to me." Then she was crying.

I took both pistols off of my hip, and held them at my sides. "I'm tired, lil cuz. This nigga got my baby, and he ain't trying to let me see her. He talking this bullshit at every turn, and Jehovah knows I just wanna body his ass. I wanna smoke this nigga like some good Loud. Fuck man."

Kamya chewed on her fingernail. "Let me do it cuz. Fuck that nigga. Teach me how to do it and I'll do it for you. I'll do anything for you." She slowly made her way over to me, and opened her arms. She hugged my waist, and rested her head on my chest. "Just teach me Phoenix, you ain't gotta feel that pain no more. We're in this shit together, if you hurt, I hurt."

I squeezed my eyelids together, and allowed the water to slide down my face. I felt sicker than a dog. I knew there was a way to use Kamya against that nigga. I saw the way he'd been looking at her every since she was thirteen years old. He wanted her. I had to figure out a way to hook him onto her line, once that happened I would be able to penetrate his pussy ass. "Aiight baby. I'ma show you what it do. I need you right now. I just need to hold you for a minute until I can gather myself. I feel like doing a bunch of way out shit right now that

I can't do. So come on, let's go back here and lay up. Put that big ass in my lap and all of that."

Kamya took my hand. "Come on. You know I got you. I can definitely do all of that." She kept holding my hand and I watched her fluffy ass cheeks jiggle, while she walked in front of me all the way to her bedroom. I wound up holding her the whole night through, with nothing but hatred in my heart for Mikey.

Chapter 5

The following morning I put ten bricks of the Rebirth in Smoke's hands. Before twelve o'clock that afternoon he and his young hittas had Orange Mound jumping like a pogo stick. Instead of there being just one line coming from one of the trap houses, there were now four of them coming from four different spots. They were so long that they looked like the lines in Great America when a bunch of people were waiting to get on a rollercoaster. He and I sat in one of the money houses in the Mound.

A money house was where the workers brought the bags of money they'd accrued after a certain number of sales. They weren't allowed to have more than a specific amount of cash them at a time. For Duffle Bag Cartel, that was ten thousand. Every time they got ten thousand dollars on them they brought the money over to the money house. Inside the house was me, and Smoke, and six armed men. Two faced the door, that had a two by four across it, with guns out. two more were in charge of guarding the back door. It also had a two by four across it, and they kept their guns out. The other two roamed the interiors of the trap looking for anything suspicious, that including noises, or whatever. All of them were given the green light to murder on sight. This house kept my livelihood in store until I came over and helped Smoke count the profits before I duffle bagged it, and took my share away.

Smoke had a big blunt in his mouth, and a stack of ten dollar bills in his hand counting them fast as a bank teller. Since the smoke was drifting upward toward his forehead, he had his right eye squinted. "Mane, I don't know what the fuck you put on that dope, homeboy, but that shit be having these feens going crazy. I ain't never made so much money in such a short amount of time in my life. I've got my rent paid up for six months in advance, my shawties rocking everything fresh and new, and I'ma cop me this lil Lexus truck from down the way later on today. All I gotta drop is fifteen for it, and he want five zips of this Rebirth. That bitch ain't even got two thousand miles on it. You know I gotta have that." He placed the stack of money in a neat pile in front of him, stood up. and took the blunt out of his mouth. "Say Mane, when we gon move on that Dragon nigga. I hear he over there making waves in Black Haven. They getting money hand over fist. If we don't do something soon they gon get so big that they're going to wind up being a serious problem. We gotta strike soon."

I finished counting my bundle. It totaled twenty eight thousand dollars in ones, tens, and twenties. My head hurt, and my finger tips felt numb. "Soon as I get back lil Potna. Let me handle this shit with this snow sunny, and when I get back we gon take a good look at them. In the mean time, you just keep getting money wit the crew. When I come back you should be every bit over a hundred gees. You feel me?"

He nodded, and sat back on the couch, picked up another wad of cash and started counting it. "You the boss Mane. I will tell you what tho. Them Black Haven boys fuckin with them Asians getting all kinds of artillery. Whenever we do go at Dragon we better be ready. They got that shit that spit rapidly. We need to step our firepower game up. I know a few niggas that a get us right." Smoke took the blunt out of his mouth, and dumped the ashes in the ashtray.

"Set that shit up and see what they got. Check them prices and if it sound good we'll fuck wit 'em. Don't let that be your primary focus though. I need you to focus on the money. We gon handle that war shit at the right time. Trust me on this." The Rebirth was rocking. I wanted and needed for us to capitalize off of its success. The more money we made in a hurry was the more I could stash. I didn't know what I would use it for off the top, but I was sure that would come to me.

"Aiight, Playboy. I'ma do just that. But I'm letting you know that if them niggas come over here on that dumb shit that me and this cartel ain't gon hesitate to wreck some shit. They don't call me Smoke for nothin. I can't wait until we wetting some shit up. I wanna see some niggas bleed man. I hate them Black Haven niggas, especially Dragon's ass." He scrunched his face, and lowered his eyes. "You heard any word about your daughter? Mikey still playing them bitch ass reindeer games?"

At the mention of Mikey's name it made me cringe. My heart started pounding fast. "That's gon be the first nigga I torture worse than I ever have before. I hate that nigga with all of my soul." I grabbed the black duffle bag from the side of the couch, and stuffed it with cash. "How much is on that table in front of you?"

"That's fifty thousand. Once I take my fifteen, it'll be thirty five." He began to separate his stash from mine. "You want me to smoke that nigga? On everythang, Mane, I'd love to do that shit, bruh."

I was grabbing the stacks of cash he pushed toward me, stuffing them inside of the bag along with the other money. "N'all, 1 don't know what's the specifics wit my daughter just yet. If we murk his ass that could be a major downfall for my baby girl. I can't risk that shit so we gon hold fast." I kept grabbing cash and stuffing it. "It's good to know that you got my back like you do though lil Homie. That's why I gotta keep you eating."

"Say Boss." One of Smoke's men said, as he looked out of the curtain toward the parking lot.

Smoke stood up. "What it do, bruh?"

"I think that's that fuck nigga Mikey truck that just pulled up across the parking lot. You want me to spray that bitch down like a can of Raid?" He asked, taking his nine millimeter off of his waist, and cocking it.

Smoke looked over to me. "Its up to you, Phoenix. We can fan this nigga down right now. I'm talking a hunnit shots. All you gotta do is say the word."

I was so close to having my lil niggas sweat him. I wanted this Nigga's life over and done with. I wanted my baby back. I wish I had known where he was keeping her. If I had, I would have killed his ass right away.

"Aw Mane, that ain't no nigga rolling that truck. That's some pregnant Bitch." He put his gun back in his hip, and allowed the curtains to fall back in place.

My phone vibrated with a text from Alicia saying that she was outside, and she needed to talk to me. She said that it was an emergency. To please not ghost her as I had been doing for the past week.

Alicia, was Mikey's wife. Prior to her marrying him, she and I had been getting down every chance we got behind his back, and even once while they were married. As cool as I was with Mikey I had a hard time staying away from his bitch because her pussy was so good, and she was so bad. After he found out about us being together on the low, and her possibly carrying my child, we fell out, and he snatched my daughter, Shanté in a act of his waging war.

I read the message on my phone, and shook my head. I really didn't feel like dealing with Alicia. There was so much other shit on my mind, already. Then again, she was pregnant with my child. I had to see what was was so urgent. I had to be there for her if she needed me.

Smoke walked to the curtains, and opened them. "That's Alicia's truck, bruh. I know she ain't over here to cop nothin.

The only person she can be looking for is you." He closed the curtain back. "You finna go fuck wit her?"

I finished packing the duffle bag with my cash, and stood up. "Yeah, I'ma fuck wit you in a few weeks. You should have more than enough work to do your thing with. If there is any serious problems you make sure you hit me up like ASAP. Aiight?"

Smoke gave me a half hug. "Bruh, I got this. Gon handle yo bidness."

***

Alicia pulled the Escalade into the parking space, and turned off the gas, but left the radio playing. Tori Kelly serenaded the interior, singing about her first love. Alicia took a deep breath and turned to me. "Phoenix why haven't you been hitting me back? I done tried to contact you on every social media platform that you got. Been hitting your phone. You just ain't fucking wit me at all huh?"

I let the seat all the way back, and closed my eyes for a second. "Shawty it ain't nothing personal. I'm just trying to get my head together. I miss my daughter like crazy. Fuckin tired of playing these games wit yo weak ass husband. Then there is Dragon laying in the weeds. Shit just been real wild for me, that's all."

"So you take it out on me? How fair is that?" She asked taking off her seat belt, and turning all the way so she could face me.

I sighed, and opened my eyes. "I should of been able to turn that pussy down. Had I been able to do that I would never be in this position. Damn I fucked up. But I'ma get I right though. Trust me on that."

Alicia was silent for a moment, taking a strand of her natural hair, and putting it behind her ears. "Phoenix, I need you.

Mikey has kicked me out into the streets. He cleared out my bank accounts, burned my clothes, and is filing for an annulment due to infidelity. He said the only reason he isn't killing me is because as much as he hates me, he hated you even more, and he's going to make you suffer. He's been beating me across the back every since you left. I want to show you my scars so bad but I'm afraid how you will react. They're horrible." She dropped her head into her lap. "I should of been strong enough to say no to you, Phoenix. I should have turned you down but I love you so much. I always have. Even before I married him."

Those were words that I didn't want to hear in that instant. All I could think about was my daughter. I missed her so bad that I was on the verge of losing my top. Alicia was a constant reminder of where my daughter was, and the price that she was paying because of me. I felt sicker than somebody struggling with food poisoning. "So what do you what from me Alicia. Huh?"

She kept her head bowed and shrugged her shoulders. "I don't know. I'm scared, broke, and alone and a few months from giving birth to your child. I guess I just need your assistance. I need you to protect me from this cold world."

"I can't even protect my daughter. How in the fuck am I going to protect you?" I imagined my baby somewhere tied up, starving, and cold. Begging for me. The mental image was killing my soul. This shit was breaking me down like a fraction.

"Just put me up for a few weeks. I'll find my way. My parents aren't messing wit me because Mikey has turned them against me. He made me seem so dirty to them, and you already know how religious they are. My father hasn't looked me in the face every since he found out that I was carrying your child. He says that I am disgrace. My mother only says that she has failed as a mother. I'm just tired of hearing all of that. She put me up for a few weeks. It shouldn't take me that long to find my next move. Whatever you give me I'll make sure I pay it back to you when I get on my feet." Alicia mumbled all of this. From the tone of her voice I could tell that she was hurt, and broken.

"Damn man." I slid out of the passenger's seat, and pulled her to the back of the truck, and held her in my arms, kissing the side of her forehead.

"You know you ain't gotta pay me back nothing. I'm just bugging right now. I got you. Whatever you need. Wherever you wanna stay, I'll take care of it. Just don't stress your pretty little heart."

She placed her face into my chest, and started to cry. "Why are you being so mean to me Phoenix? I thought you cared about me the way that I do you. I am carrying your child inside of me and its like it doesn't even matter. Its not fair." She sobbed loudly.

"Alicia, its not that I don't care. I do care about you. I have always cared about you, and that will never stop. Like I said, I just got so much on my mind that its screwing me up. You should already know I'ma hold you down though. How could I not? I know this is my fault."

Alicia held me tighter and sobbed louder. "I might know where he's keeping Shanté. In fact I am sure I do." She wiped her tears from her face.

I tensed up. "Don't play wit me Alicia. If you know where he's keeping my baby you better tell me right now."

"I think he's keeping her at the old Juke Joint on the east side of turtle creek. There is a big shack out there. Its surrounded by a big creek, and the Alligators surrounding it are big and stay hungry. I can't confirm or deny if she's really there but it won't be the first victim that he has taken there. It wasn't my business before, but it is now."

I pulled her to my chest, and held her more firmly. "I got you Alicia. I swear I do."

That night I put her up in a penthouse suite in the Hilton. I didn't know for sure what my game plan was gong to be with her, all I knew is that I couldn't leave her out on a limb. After all she was more then likely the mother of my child.

Chapter 6

Two days later, Nastia slid her hand into my lap, and interlocked her fingers inside of mine , as we flew to Moscow, Russia. Mikey sat a row in front of us drinking from a bottle of Moët, and tooting line after line of the Rebirth. The sight of this shocked the shit out of me because prior to this day I had only known him to fuck wit them Percocets, and maybe even a few Oxys from time to time, but nothing hard.

Nastia leaned into me, and rubbed her cheek against mine. "You've been so quiet baby. What's the matter?" Her blue eyes peered into my brown ones.

I was mugging the back of Mikey's head. Imagining what it would look like if I put a bullet through it. I hated that nigga worse than the Devil hated a Christian, but I was gon get his ass. I knew that without a shadow of a doubt, and when I did it was going to be lovely.

"I'm good shawty. Just sitting here taking it all in that's all." I continued to look out of the Jet's window. Images of Shanté's face roaming through my mind.

Nastia grabbed my thigh and squeezed it. "Baby, one of the main reasons I wanted you to come with me is so I could show you the other side of things. There is more to this world then just the Orange Mound. Sometimes you have to venture out into foreign lands and waters. Do you understand me? I can't stress that to you enough." She kissed the side of my neck, and licked up and down it. "I just want you to be happy baby. Trust me, there will be plenty time for you to show your anger during this trip. I have a few things in mind for you, and for Mikey that will help you gain further standings. So cheer up baby. Everything is going to be all right." She tightened her grip.

Mikey picked up his head from tooting, pulled his nose. And downed half the bottle of champagne, and laid back in the cream colored leather seat. "Can't wait until we get here, Nastia. I'm ready to cut some shit up. I always wanted to murder one of them Russian mafuckas. I don't know why, but I just do." He leaned his head down again.

"Remember Phoenix, while I am hobnobbing it will be your responsibility to make sure that Natalia is safe and sound. Watch her for me. Moscow can be a tricky place. No one can be trusted, and because of my father, and his vast enemies, I have to be sure that my daughter is in the best of hands."

"I got her. I already told you that. I ain't got no problem wetting some shit over your kid. You do what you gotta do, and I'll do the same." I went back to mugging the back of Mikey's head.

"I don't like when you're like this Phoenix. I'm already stressed enough. I'm praying that by the time we land you're in a better space. I have a lot of things planned and your attitude shouldn't be the cause of their ruin." She got up and went sat beside Mikey. They began to converse. Every now and them Mikey would look back at me with a sneer on his punk ass face.

I sat there trying to put things together in my mind. I knew that I was a long way from home. Forced to work with a mortal enemy who held the life of my daughter in the palms of his hands. This was going to be difficult for me. Nothing in my life had been easy. I would figure shit out, and prevail. I had no other choice . Shanté s life depended on it. Whatever role I had to play I would play it.

***

Natalia opened the door to the two story mansion, that was located on the east side of Moscow. Saying that my mind was blown was an understatement. She was five feet six inches tall. Light skinned, with piercing blue eyes, and long curly black hair that fell to the back of her thighs. Her lips were luscious. There was a earring on the right side of her nose. Natalia was slim up top, and down low she was built like a sista. The aroma of her perfume was heavy as the big doors swung open.

Nastia, frowned. "Didn't I tell you to never answer these fuckin doors as long as you're here? You have no idea how crazy the people that share this part of your bloodline is." Nastia snapped, and brushed past her along with her entourage of security.

Natalia rolled her eyes, and stepped to the side. "Well I told you that I didn't want to come. You insisted that I did, and because you did you should already know that I'm not going to sit around in fear. Life is too short for that." She stopped, and looked me in the eyes. "Don't I know you?"

I was the last person to step through the door. Her scent was doing some thing to me. The last time I'd seen her was in high school, and she didn't look half as good as she did right now. This girl was gorgeous. "Yeah, I think we went to school together back in the day. You were in one of the lower grades though. My name is Phoenix." I held out my hand for her.

Natalia nodded and smiled. "Yeah, now I remember. Who could ever forget such a distinctive name as that? Come on in." She looked me up and down with a sly look in her face.

Nastia peeped her from a distance. "You can stop looking at him like that. Your father is his uncle. That makes you family. Since you have such a hard time dealing with the men I appoint to look after you, he's going to take on those duties. Hopefully you will be respectful." She came and took a hold of my hand, and led me through the mansion.

We wound up in her master's bedroom. It was huge. All white, with a chandelier hanging from the ceiling. The bed was in the middle of the floor, with thin, pink, veils covering the expanse of it. There was a big screen television inside of the wall. A Jacuzzi to the left of the doorway, twenty steps from the massive bathroom. To my right was a small swimming pool, a short ways from it was a balcony that overlooked the night skyline of Moscow. It smelled of jasmine.

Nastia closed the big double doors, and casually stepped over to me. She rubbed along my chest, and sucked on her bottom lip as she looked into my eyes. "Are you feeling any better baby?"

I smiled. "Yeah, I'm good. I just gotta figure some shit out. That's all."

"Why don't you tell me what it is. Don't you know that I could help you?" She asked stroking the side of my cheek.

I stepped away from her. "I'm good. We already made a deal. I'ma be out here wit you for two weeks. I'ma make sure that Natalia is safe and sound. Gon bust a few moves for you. Then, when we get back everything gon go back to normal. A deal is a deal."

"Ugh. You're so fucking stubborn. I don't know what to do wit you right now." She crossed her arms like a little girl, mugged me, and shook her head. "I have a business meeting of sorts tonight. I'll be out for a few hours. My security team will keep the perimeter sealed, and surveilled. You do the best you can to not get into an argument with Natalia. That girl has a sharp tongue. She's going to push your buttons left and right so you better be ready. Remember that she is my heart, and I appreciate you for looking after her." She stepped back in front of me, and closed her eyes. "Can I have a kiss until I see you later?"

I leaned down and kissed her thin lips, pulled her into my embrace, then grabbed a hold of her ass. Her tongue tried to enter into my mouth, but I avoided it by turning my head side ways.

Nastia broke the kiss. "This palace is yours. Feel free to get comfortable. The remote is right there. I'll see you in a few hours. I'm taking Mikey along with me. I have some unofficial business for him to handle tonight." She made her way toward the double doors, stopped, smiled back at meme and blew a kiss. Then she was gone.

I took the remote control and turned on the television to the Unites States Sports Center. Took my leather Sean Jean off and tossed it on the bed. By the time I got down to my beater there was a knock on the bedroom door. "Man, who is it?"

The door swung inward and Natalia appeared in a pair of cut off, blue jean, daisy dukes, and a pink beater that conformed to the upper portion of her body.

"Who do you think it is? It's cousin Natalia." She giggled, and stepped all the way into the room. Placed her back in the door. Her thick thighs jiggled.

I glanced at her. "What you doing in here, shawty?"

She tapped on her chin with a finger. "Hmm, let me see. All of the security is outside of the house, and my mother, whose always all up by ass, left me in this lonely mansion with a fine ass man that I used to have a crush on in high school. I got on these little shorts. Ain't had a chance to be alone with a male for almost a year. You tell me?" She gave me a devilish look. "Are you really my father's nephew?"

I shrugged my shoulders. "As far as I know. Why?"

50

She stepped away from the door and came toward me. With each step that she took her thighs shook. She was barefoot . Her small, pretty toes were painted pink. This bitch was bad.

"I don't know, I guess I'm just curious because I've never gotten the chance to meet him before. Any man with his blood is fascinating to me." She stepped up to me, and looked into my eyes. "What was my father like? My mother says he was a legend?"

"Shid, I don't know. I'm only a few years older than you. Yo pops was well before my time. I'm sure all of the stories that you've heard are the same ones that I have."

She stared off dreamily. "My mother says he was some guy. I wish I could have met him. I'd rather to have been raised by my father then my mother any day. The black side of me is so thirsty." Natalia sighed. And looked up to me. "Are you screwing my mother?"

"If you mean fucking then yeah. I hit that old pussy every now and then. Why? That make you mad or something?" I laughed and sat in the bed while watching the scores on the bottom of the screen go past.

"Oh no. Mad is the last thing I am. You see, you're going to be looking after me for the next fourteen days. I can guarantee you that we'll be fuckin by tomorrow. If not tonight." She unbuttoned the top of her Daisy Dukes and unzipped them. I caught a glimpse of the pink lace panties underneath.

"Shawty didn't you just hear your mama tell you who I am to you? I'm yo family girl. Fall back."

Natalia shook her head. "Oh no. You see my mama be having those security guards all up my ass. I've haven't had a chance to get any relief, and those guys that she has watching over me don't do it for me. Nall Phoenix. I got some shit in me that calls out for you. I don't know what it is but I'm aching down here." She ran her fingers over the split in her jeans and did this sexy lil moan. Her nipples poked through her beater.

I felt my dick getting hard as hell. It was throbbing and everything. Nastia had made it perfectly clear that she was crazy about her daughter. I didn't know what all that meant, but I wasn't willing to risk whatever fucking with Natalia would bring. Because of Nastia I had Orange Mound jumping. A nigga was making money hand over fist. I was on my way to establishing myself in the game after I took care of a little business out here for her. There was no way I'd jeopardize my standings for a piece of pussy. I was smarter then that.

Natalia pulled her shorts down far enough to expose her bald, plump pussy lips. They had to be the fattest lips that I had ever seen in my life. She ran her finger through the middle of them. "You have no idea how hot this pussy is Phoenix. Its young. It's fresh. Its connected to you. You can't tell me that you don't want any." Natalia slid the finger into her self, and pulled it out, walking toward me with it. She stepped in between my legs. "Here you go. Just taste me."

I laughed. "Shawty get yo lil ass out of here. I ain't fucking wit you on that level." My dick was really jumping in my pants now. Her scent was driving me nuts. I felt my twisted roots getting the better of me.

She slid her hand over my lap and squeezed my dick. "Damn. You're so hard. I wanna see it so bad. I'm curious to see what my black side looks like." She rubbed all over my dick before she leaned her head down and kissed the jeans.

I involuntarily humped upward into her mouth before I caught myself and pushed her away.

"Gon Natalia. I got a lot of respect for your mother. I ain't gon do her like that."

She unbuttoned my jeans, and unzipped them. "I just want to see what it looks like. Please. I never got a chance to meet my father. But I've heard all of the stories about our family. They drive me nuts. I wish I was raised by him. Wish things were different." She pulled my dick out, and her eyes got bucked. "Oh my God. I've only seen white ones. This is crazy." She sniffed the big head. Kissed it, and started to stroke it up and down. "Can I try something? Please?"

My dick started jumping in her hand. The more firmly she held it, the longer it grew until it looked like a mini baseball bat in her yellow hand. I smacked her hand away and scooted back. "N'all, we ain't finna do this shit, shawty." I jumped up and pulled my pants up. My dick's head peeked out of my waistband.

She continued to pursue me. "Seriously, Phoenix. What's so good about my mother, but you'll pass on me?" She asked, looking offended.

I got my pants in order, and dusted off my shirt. "Shawty yo mama on bidness. Far as I can see you ain't on shit. That fine shit can only go so far. I will give you that though." I appraised her one last time, noticing how hard her nipples were and the way her shorts were all up in her gap That shit made me shudder involuntarily, before walking to the big doors and opening them. There was no doubt in my mind. I would fuck her senseless if ever I got between her thighs.

Natalia looked dumbfounded. "Seriously?"

"Seriously, Shawty. I'ma fuck wit you later." I held the door open wide enough for her to step through it.

Natalia's nostrils flared, as she shook her head. She'd stopped directly in front of me, and smiled as she looked into my eyes. "Looks can be deceiving Phoenix. I am more than what you think I am. You'll find that out real soon. In regards to this though." She cupped my piece, and squeezed it until it grew. This made her run her long tongue across her lips. "I see how hard I make you Phoenix. You won't be able to turn me down forever. I'm going to see what this is all about. I am sure of that." She kissed my lips softly, and stepped past me with her long hair flowing behind her. She looked like a Goddess. Her shorts were all up in her ass so much so that her cheeks were exposed.

All I could do was shake my head, until the scent of her perfume went away. My piece was throbbing like crazy. I kept seeing Natalia's piercing blue eyes. She intrigued me. I wanted to know what more there was to her, if anything. What was it that she had up her sleeve? I was sure that it wouldn't be long before I found out.

Chapter 7

"Aiight Phoenix, now she done broke this move down to us three times already. This shit simple and sweet. We gon go in here and fuck over some shit Memphis style, Mane. She said no guns, and I'm cool wit that. You cool wit that?" Mikey asked, before shaking up his pink Sprite, and turning it up.

I slid the leather gloves onto my hands, then rolled down my white ski mask. We were parked behind a Heating and Air condition company, in the north side if Moscow. It was two in the morning their time, and I was ready to get this move over with. Nastia had three marks that she wanted us to lay down. She'd said that it was important that we fuck them over, and leave them twisted in a way that would bring prestige to her name. Supposedly, they needed to be knocked out of the way before she was able to move forward in whatever she was trying to accomplish. I didn't know exactly what that was specifically, but I was sure that it would help me to advance in the game down the line, so I was all for it. I still couldn't get Natalia's strapped ass off of my mind. When Nastia had gotten back later that same day I'd tore her pussy up imagining that I was fucking her daughter.

"Nigga you gonna say somethin or what?" Mikey mugged.

I looked over the knives inside of the pocket of fatigue . The handles were made for hunters. The blades were serrated. I was good to go. Killing something is definitely what I needed. "Say I'm cool Mane. Using a knife ain't never stopped me from taking a nigga out the game Potna. Let's handle this bidness. Seem like that's our cue right there."

A female with long red hair appeared on the cobble stone road that we were parked She took a cigarette out of her purse, and sparked it before she started to walk toward us. The wind view through her hair, causing it to wave like a flag. When she reached the van she knocked on the door three times and kept on walking. That was the cue that Nastia said we'd be given. It was time to roll.

"Let's do it."

We jumped out of the van, and bent over as low as we could. Jogging down the cobble street and toward the back door to the business. The woman had left the door wide open. I rushed inside of it, and the first thing I heard was Russian music blaring out of the speakers. The door lead into a dark hallway. It smelled like salty and super sugary foods were being cooked. I took the hallway until it led to a sales room where both heating, and air conditioner systems were lined up. The room was carpeted. It felt soft to the bottoms of my shoes. I jogged past that one, through the next room. Then I could smell cigars. A bunch of arguing ensued. The pathway leading up to the next room was dimly lit, but as we came off of it the lights turned blue. Smoke welcomed us before I was able to see anybody. There were hanging beads covering the entry way. I paused and peeked inside it. There were three men sitting at a round table counting stacks and stacks of American money.

Mikey came inside. He paused and looked, then shot forward pulling a big knife from his waistband. The beads sounded. He rushed to the far end of the table. Mikey grabbed one of the fat Russians by his forehead, sliced his throat and slung him to the floor, and attacked the second one.

I ran through the beads. The man closest to me stood up to pull his weapon. He aimed it at Mikey, and a part of me wanted to allow him to kill Mikey in cold blood so I could be rid of him but I had to think about Shanté. Mikey's death was also death to my daughter. I couldn't allow that to happen. I raised the serrated blade and slammed it into the attempted shooter's spine as hard as I could.

56

He yelled and dropped the gun before standing straight up, and trying to turn around. Suddenly the knife was going in and out of him, punching his soft flesh again and again. The Russian threw a weak elbow that missed. He fell backward on top of the table, struggling for dear life.

My knife plunged again and again. His blood shot into the air, splashing the table repeatedly. Mikey ran and stood over him. "Oh, you was gone shoot me? Huh? Huh?" His eyes were wild. He the man's hair, p laced his blade under his neck and sliced it. Mikey slammed his head into the table as hard as he could. *Bam*! "Bitch ass nigga!"

Another one of them crawled around on the floor. Dragging himself by his elbows. He left a trail of blood under him. "Uh. Uh." He dared to look toward us. There were two bloody holes in his back.

I stood over him and placed my shoe on his neck , forcing him to the floor where he continued to struggle for dear life. This Boscoe?" I asked Mikey.

Mikey came over and ripped the man's jacket from his body. Then he cut his shirt down the middle, until he exposed the red, white, and blue flag on his back. "Hell yeah dis his bitch ass, Mane. Shawty say she want his head cut off his shoulders, and I ain't got no problem doing that." He knelt beside the man. Smacked him in the back of the head. "Say Homeboy, you know how much yo head worth right now?" He asked, them grabbed a handful of his hair.

"Please. Please. I beg of you. Don't do this to me. I'll make you two very rich men." Boscoe pleaded.

Mikey took his head and slammed it into the floor. "A! Shut the fuck up, Mane. You ain't finna make us shit. We already getting paid for the bounty on yo head nigga."

"I have Yen. I have Euros. I have American. I'll give you five million in each. Just please, don't kill me."

"Man body his bitch ass and get it over with. We gotta get out of here. Fuck is you waiting on?" I snapped ready to get down and handle him myself if need be. I always had this timer in my head to do a job. Whenever things got past a few minutes it started to go off louder and louder with each passing second.

"Hold on Mane. Dis mafucka just basically said he'll give us fifteen million. Now I don't know about you but I want that kind of scratch." He picked dude up by the hair. "Say fuck nigga. How you gon give us this cash Potna? Speak up!"

"I'll wire it. Just give me your account number. You'll have it in a matter of minutes. I swear." He said this with a strained voice.

"You hear that homeboy? He saying we'll be millionaires in a natter of minutes. I can't pass that up. Get yo Bitch ass up." Mikey stood up, and started to pull the man to his feet.

"Aw! Fuck!" He struggled against him. Blood gushed out of the holes in his back. "Aw. Aw. My fuckin." He reached into his pocket, and pulled out a phone. "One phone call. Just one and the money is yours."

Mikey nodded. "Hell yeah I like the sound of that.

The man began to text rapidly on his phone. He wrote in Russian so I couldn't understand what he was writing, but I feared the worst. Besides, there had to be a reason that Nastia needed him out of the equation. I didn't know why, but he must of posed a threat to our future success, and I couldn't let that remain.

"What? Nigga hell n'all. Fuck that?" I took the knife and slammed it into the side of Boscoe's neck, stabbing him as hard as I could before letting him drop to the ground.

"What the fuck is you doing, nigga? That was our meal ticket right there." Mikey hollered looking down at him.

"Fuck dude. There gotta be a reason that Nastia wanted him dead. Come on, let's get the fuck out of here."

I heard a door slam, then heavy foot steps on the floor. The next thing I knew two dudes appeared dressed in all white fatigues. They had assault rifles in their hands. When they saw us they knelt down, and began to fire. *Pop*! *Pop*! *Pop! Pop!*

Them bullets were whizzing past me so close that I could hear them as they traveled past. I flipped over the table. It absorbed about ten shots. I was glad that I had used my instincts, and never left home without my banger. I pulled the Glock off of my hip and got to blasting back at their bitch asses. *Boom. Boom. Boom.*

They ducked and scattered back into the hallway from whence they'd come. They sent ten more shots in our direction. I responded with three more. Mikey jumped up and took off running out the way that we'd come leaving me in the lurch.

I busted four more times. Boom. Boom. Boom. Boom. Then followed his path. When I got outside and to the van he was just pulling off. I ran as fast as I could as the bullets from the enemy wet up the side of the van we were driving. The old bullet wound in my right thigh was paining me. In just the knick of time I grabbed a hold of the passenger's door, and pulled it open. Jumped inside of it, and punched Mikey straight in his jaw, hard. *Bam*!

The van swerved. It jumped a curb before he straightened it out, and stepped on the gas.

More bullets riddled us. The passenger's window shattered. I could see the dents forming inside of the body. One of the tires exploded and went flat.

I punched Mikey's ass again. *Bam.* "You bitch ass nigga, you was gone leave me back there to get killed. And after I stopped dude from killing yo punk ass only a few minutes ago? What type of shit is that?" I snapped. I leaned out of the window, and let my Glock ride back to back. Boom. *Boom. Boom. Boom.* It went empty. I released the magazine from its body, took an extra clip out of my pocket, and slammed it into the body of my gun and got to yacking at their asses until Mikey bent the corner. Blood was dripping from Mikey's mouth.

When we were well out of the vicinity. He pulled the van over, and rushed me, swinging wildly. "Pussy ass nigga. You got to fuck my wife, and bust my shit." He was swinging wildly as hard as he could.

I as ready for his ass. I took two of his blows, before I opened the passenger's door, and made us fall on to the concrete on purpose. Once there, I got on top of his ass and started hitting him with blow after blow. I knew I was fucking him up because every time I hit his ass all he could do was groan in pain. His mask could only prevent a little bit of the pain.

Mikey grabbed me, and we began to roll around on the concrete. "Let me up nigga. Let me up or I swear to God you'll never see your daughter again. Her or Toya."

Bitch ass nigga. He never could fuck wit my bidness. My hands were lethal. Always had been. I released him and jumped up. "Nigga you was finna leave me back there. You was finna let them punk ass Russians kill me, and right after I saved yo fuckin life. What type of shit is that?" I snapped with my heart beating like crazy in my chest.

He got up staggering around on the cobbled street. Behind us were three more pubs, aparking lot, and a big church. I thought it was odd to have a church, and a few bars on the same street, but apparently they didn't think so in Moscow.

"I wasn't gone leave you. I was just getting the van ready. You should of never busted me in my shit. Fuck!" He spit out a wad of blood on the concrete.

"Nigga on everythang mane, if you ain't have my daughter I would of knocked yo shit out. I would of never pulled that fuck shit boy." I was heated.

He wiped his mouth. His lips were swollen from my punches. "Fuck you nigga. Yousa snake, ain't no telling what you a do, but I don't put shit pass you. That's fa damn sho." He bent over and spit on the sidewalk again.

I rushed over and jacked him up. "I wanna talk to Shanté, man. Let me talk to my baby girl. I'm going crazy without her."

He balled up his face, and knocked my hands away. "Get the fuck off me boy! Fuck wrong wit you. I don't owe you a muthafuckin thang whether you saved my life a not. You still crossed me. You lucky Shanté still alive. You know how we get down back home, bruh. Ain't shit changed, nigga. Let's go!" He bumped me, and jumped back into the busted down van.

With every fiber of my being I wanted to put two into his back. This bitch ass nigga had me by the balls. I was missing Shanté worse than ever, and I was concerned that my baby was no longer alive. I didn't know how much longer I could put up with his bullshit and his fuck boy ways, it was taking a toll on me. I missed my Princess.

Ghost

Chapter 8

"Phoenix come on. Will you get your ass in already?" Natalia asked sitting in the red drop top Porsche, looking past me and toward the big mansion. "My mom said the only way I'm going shopping is if you tag alone, so come on and let's go." The sun reflected off of her shiny forehead. It felt like it was every bit of eighty degrees out side with very little wind.

I stood in the long drive way in a black and gray, Gucci short set, over matching Airmax ninety fives. I had a fitted cap on to the back, and two diamond studs in my ear.

"Shawty you already know that if I roll off wit yo ass it ain't gon do nothing but get both of us in trouble. You got on that short ass Fendi skirt too. Got them thick ass thighs out and thangs. Mane its only so much a nigga can take." I laughed, even though I was serious as hell though.

She smiled her. "We family remember? We ain't on none of that bullshit, I thought. I promise I'll be a good girl. We're just spending family time. Cross my heart." She slid her finger across her B cup breasts. The swells glistened as if she'd used some kind of skin care product that had glitter inside of it. I could smell her perfume from where she sat and it was enough to make my piece twinge.

Nastia appeared, and walked from the house. She slid her arm around my lower back, and kissed my cheek. "Hey Phoenix, why are you guys still here?"

Natalia lowered her eyes, and looked irritated. "He was just inquiring about where all I wanted to go. Its nothing. We're figuring it out. Go back into the mansion. Jeez."

Nastia, stepped to the side of me. "Natalia, you know I don't like when you talk to me like that. Now show me some respect. I demand it." She implored, stomping her foot.

Natalia rolled her eyes. "Sorry mom. But hey look, we got this. We're good. I'll see you in a few hours. Cool?"

Nastia slid her arm back around my waist. She leaned into my ear. "Hey, I could tag along if you want me to. Its really up to you."

"Mom please. Jesus Christ! I've been deprived of that side of my family all of my life. Just let us be. I'll see you in a few hours."

Nastia sighed. She looked up at me, and kissed my cheek. "Okay then, you guys be safe. I'll see you in about four hours. That enough time for you Natalia?"

"Yeah." She opened up her passenger's door, and patted the seat for me. "Come on Phoenix, let's roll out."

Nastia handed me a black card. "Get her whatever she wants, and you can get whatever you want as well. I'ma miss you." She kissed the side of my mouth, and made her way back inside of the mansion.

I jumped into the passenger's seat and closed the door. Before she pulled off I adjusted the seat so that it fit my length, threw my seat belt around me, and rested my arm on the window sill. "Let's ride shawty."

Natalia put the Porsche into gear, and pulled out of the driveway. There was a smile on her face as she reached over and wiped her mother's kiss off of me.

"I still can't understand how you could let her kiss all on you, but hat's none of my business. I'm just happy to get some alone time with you." She sped out of the driveway, and along the winding road.

"Aw yeah, what type of shit you got in mind besides this whole shopping thing?" My eyes went down and saw how the hem of her short skirt had risen just a tad. Most of her thighs were exposed. They were thick and golden. Damn she was so strapped, it was crazy.

"Well." She made a left turn, and pulled out of the wooded area then took another road that led to a highway, and got on it.

"I was thinking that you and I have a nice lil picnic. Chat a little bit and get to know each other. I mean we are family. I want to ask you some questions, and I'm sure there are things that you want to know about me. Isn't there?"

"Not really. From as far as I can see you a spoiled lil bitch, that's still sucking at her mother's breast. I'm not impressed shawty. Ain't no sense of fuckin wit you when I can fuck wit yo mama and get everythang that I need out of her. Fucking wit you is like fucking wit a unnecessary middle man."

I sat back, and enjoyed the breeze that was coming on to my face. I knew that my words were harsh but I needed to fuck with her brain a lil bit. I didn't want her to think that she could get by with me just because she was bad. N'all, I was over that. Fuckin a bad bitch was a regular for me. Now days a bitch had to have more than just a pretty face and a nice body. They had to be on their shit. She had to be able to benefit me and my advancement in some sort of way."

"Damn, that's harsh. Where is your compassion?" She asked looking over to me.

I shrugged my shoulders. 'That shit died a long time ago."

She drove for a few seconds. "Phoenix there is more to me that meets the eye. If you are familiar with our blood line then you should already know that I have that boss shit in me. My father was a legend. And so is my mother. They came together to make me which means that I have to either be as good as them, or ten times better than them. I choose to be the latter." She licked her sexy lips, and sped past another car on the highway and got behind a semi truck, before swerving around it and flooring the Porsche.

I peeped Natalia from the corner of my eye. There seemed to be a certain confidence about her that was turning me on. "How you gon be that?"

"I have my plans in place. Everything will happen when its supposed too. Until then I'm going to play my role because I do it so well." She smiled again. Her dimples appearing on both cheeks. She definitely favored Taurus when she made certain faces. There was no denying that she was his daughter. "But what about you? Are you looking to be working under my mother for the rest of your life?" She eased off of the gas at the sight of a highway trooper up ahead.

"Hell n'all. I'm my own man. Your mother is a crutch for me. I respect her slot, and by using it I'll be able to advance into where I need to be. I refuse to be anybody's worker for the rest of my life. I'm a boss by blood, just like you are."

Natalia nearly broke her neck to look over at me. She took a deep breath, and exhaled loudly before switching lanes again.

"Phoenix, how was it growing up? Is our roots as twisted as my mother makes it seem?" She asked just above a whisper.

"What do you mean?"

"Like with my father, Taurus? Did he really have something going on with his mother?"

"That's what I heard. Ain't nobody in the family deny it's or make a big deal about it either, so I guess so. Why would you ask me that?"

"I don't know, I was just curious to know because that seems so far fetched. What would make a man turn to his mother in that way? And vice versa? Things must of really been rough for the both of them, huh?"

I nodded. "I guess so. Like I said before, I'm just a few years older than you. Taurus is before my time."

"Yeah I know. But what about you though?"

"What about me?"

Natalia took an exit ramp before stopping at the lights briefly, and making a left   and rolling down the road that led to the biggest mall in Moscow. Once inside she parked the Porsche, and turned off the engine.

"I mean have you done anything with anybody in our family? You know, on that level?" Her eyes peered into mine hungrily. As if she was dying to hear about an experience from my past. There were so many that traveled through my mind. I didn't know where to begin.

"Natalia, our family is crazy. Our bloodline has its issues with boundaries, or the lack there of. All that forbidden shit that you're feeling inside of you comes from our half. You will never be able to control it. You can only hope to suppress it, trust me."

She began breathing hard. Her face was flushed. "Phoenix, I need you to touch me right now. Please. My panties are soaked, and I'm throbbing like crazy down there." Her heavy breathing increased. She opened her thick thighs, and arched her back. The hem of her skirt moved backward on her hips exposing the crotch of her red, lace, panties. "Touch me. Please Phoenix."

I slid my hand along that hot thigh, and squeezed it. Then I trailed it sideways until I came into contact with her middle. Once there, I rubbed her material, felt the thick lips, and smushed the panties inside of them. My middle finger traced a path up and down her lower lips.

Natalia threw her head back. "Tell me I'm your lil cousin. Tell me I'm apart of the family. Please Phoenix. I need to hear it." She reached in between her legs, and yanked her panties to the side. Her cleft appeared, wet and engorged. She licked her fingers and spread the sopping lips.

I moved her hand out of the way. Her scent began to rise to my nostrils. I played over her pussy. Felt one lip, and then the other. I opened them far enough so I could see her clitoris. Then I was pinching it, and running my thumb in a circle around it.

She jerked. "Aww, yes. Touch me Phoenix. Touch me there. I'm your family."

I slid two fingers into her as deep as I could. Her pussy felt hot and tight. Juices dripped out of her hole. I pulled them out and sucked them into my mouth. Tasted her essence, then I was fingering her again, this time at full speed.

She threw her head back, and humped into my hand, . harder and harder. "Uh, you're my family. You're my family. Yes. Ooo. Fuck! Yes! I'm cumming Phoenix. I'm cumming!" She screamed and clamped her thighs over my hand. Shaking like crazy. Her nipples poked through her Fendi top. I rubbed all over he flat stomach and fingered her belly button ring, then I was back in her pussy again fucking in and out while she bounced up and down on my digits. Before she could cum again I placed the wet fingers on her lips, and watched her lick all over them , grabbed a handful of her hair, and right in the parking lot I tongued her down, while I rubbed all over her bald, yellow, pussy.

"Let me suck that black dick Phoenix. Let me suck it right here and right now. I don't give a fuck who sees." She reached over and unzipped my pants, and began to work my dick out of it.

I glanced around the parking lot, there were a few people going to their cars with bags in their hands. Others were pulling up preparing to go inside the mall. This was dangerous. We were in a drop top in Moscow. Anybody could have looked over and saw what was taking place.

Natalia had my piece out, licking up and down it. She pumped it five times, and held it in her tiny fist, before sucking it into her mouth. She moaned around it. "Its sooooo big." She said, with it still inside of her mouth. Suddenly she was sucking me like a porn star. Her lips traveled up and down at a fast pace. She added lots of spit and slurped it back up. Natalia was a beast. My eyes rolled into the back of my head a few times. I found myself humping up from the seat so I could get deeper into her mouth. She pumped me with her fist and sucked and sucked until I couldn't hold it no more. Just as a few blond females walked toward us with a bunch of shopping bags in their hands, I tensed up and felt my seed spilling out of me and into her mouth. "Arrgh." I hollered and came hard.

She sucked harder, pumped me slower, and methodically squeezed as much of my seed out of me as she could. Natalia swallowed it all then licked all over the head. "You're my blood. My family. We taste so good."

***

Twenty minutes later, I watched her try on fifty different outfits, and that didn't include stiletto heels, and other forms of shoes. One thing I had to give Natalia her props on was the fact that she knew how to dress, and had swag. We wound up spending forty thousand dollars in Moscow's version of Sak's Fifth Ave, and then another ten grand in Victoria Secrets where I watched Natalia model one piece of lingerie after the next. She ended up getting me so hot with one red number, that I wound up following her into the dressing room, making her put her foot up on the chair, and squatting between her thighs. I opened her pussy lips and sucked on her clit while she rode my face like a savage.   One of the sales girls broke up our party before I could get her off.

After shopping, we wound up at the lake front, sitting on a towel on the sand. Natalia'd brought along a wooden picnic basket. It was filled with all kinds of sandwiches, potato chips, snacks and drinks. She sat across from me with her long hair blowing in the wind. "Phoenix, what if I told you that you didn't need my mother to advance in the game?

That all you needed was me? What would you say?" She placed two sandwiches on a paper plate, with some chips, and handed them to me.

"I'd say you need to elaborate. Right now your mother got me plugged in all of the areas that I need to be plugged into. I got a lot of starving niggas back in Memphis that depend on me to feed their family, and the way I'm able to do that right now is because of your mother, so unless you're talking some serious numbers, you need to shut that shit up."

Her nostrils flared. "You need to shut the fuck up Phoenix, and hear me out. Damn. Don't let this light skin fool you. I'm still a sista. Our blood is still one in the same." She grabbed a pink lemonade, and twisted the top off of it.

"Aright, well let me hear you out. Go ahead and speak."

"N'all, now is not the right time. But you'll see what I'm talking about. But answer my question, if all you needed was me in order to advance in the game, would you cut her completely off, and solely fuck wit me? That's the question. I need an answer."

I leaned back on me elbows and surveyed the beach. It was packed. Every where I looked there seemed to be a fine ass white girl with a G string up her backside. Typically, snow bunnies weren't my thing, but Russia had some of the baddest snow bunnies I'd ever seen in all of my life. They weren't all that skinny either. N'all, these white girls had meat in their bones. Fat asses and all of that shit. Looking over the beach was like a white version of the Player's Club. "Say shawty, if you was able to make shit happen on your own I would kick ya moms to the curb like a-sap. I mean I got mad love for her but you and I are family right?"

She smiled. "That's right."

"Then just like Taurus would, I would ride wit my family before anybody else. It can be me and you. I just gotta know what path you're traveling down. I got a whole army that eat off of my plate. If I ever put my faith in you, you'd have to really show your ass baby. I believe you could. Its something in your eyes that's telling me that.

She climbed onto all fours, and crawled across the beach towel. Her face was a inch way from mine. Those pretty blue eyes were gorgeous. "You gave me the answer that I needed to hear. Now just chill and I'm going to handle my business. You'll see." She kissed my lips. As she held the side of my face, her tongue danced all over mine. I didn't know what she had up her sleeve, but something in my soul told me that it was going to be good.

Ghost

Chapter 9

"Argh! Argh! Argh! The bald, red faced Russian yelled at the top of his lungs.

I took the index finger on his right hand, and snapped it, just like I had his pinky finger, ring finger and his middle finger. All of them were broken with the bones sticking out of the sides of them.

Nastia had him chained to the wall in her dungeon. Sweat dripped from his face, and off of his chin. She walked up to him, and stroked his cheek. "Are you going to sign over your shares. I need an answer now."

" You don't know what you're doing Nastia. I swear. I was a loyal partner to your father. We made millions together. Its because of me that you are so wealthy. I am not Boscoe. I would never screw you over. You don't have to get rid of me." He declared. "You don't have to do this."

She grabbed his face with her left hand. "You insufferable son of a bitch. Answer the fucking question. Are you going to sign over your shares to me, or will the signings come from your wife? I'm sure she'll be happy to step in and handle this side of the business. Will you or not?!" She slapped him as hard as she could.

He hawked and spit a loogie into her face. It splashed against her forehead, and rolled off of her nose. "You ungrateful, rich, bitch. You think because you let your old man treat you as his common whore that you're going to take over a pharmaceutical company that I've worked so hard to build from the ground up. One that is worth billions. Well if you think that you can kiss my ass. I mean really fucking kiss it. You're nothin more than Serge's leftovers, his trash." He spit again. This time it landed on her Prada dress.

I grabbed him by the throat, and slammed the knife into his shoulder. I twisted it in a full circle, and shoved it deeper until it hit his bone. I could feel the steel scraping against. It encouraged me to inflict even more pain.

"Arghgggg!" He stomped his feet, and fought against the chains that had him bound.

Nastia wiped the spit from her face with a handkerchief. Then she removed the excess amount from her dress. She mugged him. "So, we're going to go this route are we? Okay." took three times back, and looked over to me. "Take off those ears. He seems as if he can't hear what I am asking him to do anyway."

"No problem." I returned.

"No. No. No." He hollered.

I held his forehead, and slammed it backward into the brick wall , sliced both of his ears lobes off simultaneously, and dropped them to the floor. With a wicked smile I took a step back and admired my work.

"Argggh! Argggh!" Blood ran from the sides of his face, and along his neck in thick globs. He choked on his own spit, and began to cough loudly.

Nastia bent over and pulled some paperwork out of a brief-case that she'd brought along with her. "Olaf, I have the papers right here. All I need you to do is to sign the paperwork and we'll be on about our business. Sounds easy enough, right?" Her heels tapped on the floor as she made her way back over to him.

Blood poured out of his ears like red maple syrup. He yelled at her in Russian. Olaf snapped out, fighting against the chains again with no success. "You bitch, you have no idea how many things our company is tied to. We have to answer not only to Putin here in Russia, but the powers that be way up on the totem pole of the middle east, and the United States.

We fix elections you dumb girl. All you see is money. It'll be the death of you." He slumped against the chains, and snapped. "Let me the fuck out of here!"

"So does that mean that you're going to sign the papers, orrrrrr....." She asked.

Even I had to laugh at that. But now at least things were starting to make sense for me. Nastia was in pursuit of a billion dollar pharmaceutical company. We were in Russian so she could knock off the share holders of her father's company. I only wondered why she'd chosen to use me and Mikey to lay the bastards down? She could've just as easily used any of her trained assassins to handle the jobs, but for some reason she'd chosen to use me and him. I needed to get to the bottom of that.

"Over my dead body. You hear me, bitch?! Over my fuckin dead body!" He spat.

Nastia shrugged her shoulders. "As you wish." She nodded at me.

I took a deep breath and stood in front of him. His eyes were as big as saucers. I looked back at Nastia. "Its a wrap?"

"Its a wrap, baby. Finish him." She replaced the papers into the briefcase, and stood back so she could watch me dead his ass.

I stepped forward, and went on a rampage, stabbing him over and over. In the stomach. In the chest. In the neck. In the face. Over and over, imagining that he was Mikey. The blade tore his muscles and tissues. He coughed up a bunch of blood and started to gag.

I stood back. My blade dripping blood, all over the ground.

Nastia stepped along side him and shook her head. "What a waste. Luckily for us in Moscow a wife can sign for her husband. They are viewed as one complete entity. You won't have any problems signing over these documents will you now Romana?"

Mikey yanked the tape off of her mouth, and flung her to the floor. "Speak bitch."

"No. I'll sign them. I'll sign them right now." She swore.

Mikey grabbed a handful of her hair, and yanked her to her feet causing her to scream. He slammed her against the brick wall. Placed his forehead against hers. "After you sign these papers you will keep your mouth shut for at least a month. Do you hear me?"

"Yes. I swear. I won't utter a word." She assured.

Nastia smiled, and handed her the pen. "Here you go Sweetie. Sign your name on the bottom line, and his should go at the top. So sorry for the inconvenience, but business is business.

***

Two hours later as I was showering and washing the blood off of me, there was a knock on the door, and then it swung inward. I peeked out of the shower curtain to see Mikey's punk ass face. "Say bruh, I'm in here, Mane. I'll be out in a few minutes."

"Nigga I know you in here. Damn. If you'd shut the fuck up for a minute maybe you'd see my reason for coming in here right now. Huh." He handed his phone toward me.

I though the was trying to set me up. Knew it couldn't be anybody on the phone other than Alicia. "I'm showering, Mane. Ain't nobody on that bitch I wanna talk to." I waved him off, and closed the shower curtain back. "I'll be out in a minute, Mane."

"Its Shanté's birthday in two days Potna. I just thought since you saved a nigga from a bullet a few days ago that the least I could do was allow you to talk to your baby girl. After all, she is innocent in all of this."

I yanked the curtain back open, and dried my face with my left hand. "Are you shitting me, Bruh?"

He shook his head. "N'all, enjoy your call Mane. We got some shit we need to talk about before we leave Moscow too, bruh. This experience has been eye opening for me." He handed me the phone and stepped out of the bathroom.

I felt the tears slide down my face right away. I placed the phone to my ear. "Hello, baby, is that you?"

"Daddy. Daddy, where are you?" Shanté cried.

"I'm right here lil momma. Daddy is right here. I miss you so so much baby." Damn I was crying.

She began to sob. "I miss you too daddy. I wanna come home with you. I don't like it here. Everybody is so mean." She cried even harder. "Can you come and get me? Please? I promise I'll be good. I won't mess up no more."

I was crying so hard that my eyes were burning. I was shaking. "Baby listen to me, I'm coming to get you in a few days. Can you be strong for me until then? Please mommas?" Man this was hurting my heart. I knew my daughter needed me. I wanted to kill Mikey in the worst way for putting her through this. She was just a baby in my eyes. She always would be. My baby. My first child. I loved her with all my heart and soul.

"A few days is a long long time daddeee?" More crying. "Why can't you just come and get me right now? I don't want to be here. I hate it here!" She screamed and started to cough, and cry loudly.

Now I was in the bathroom on my knees. My head lowered, breaking down worse that I ever had in my entire life. I felt sicker than a dog. "Baby, I'm coming. Just please be strong for me. Please. I need you to be as strong as possible and I will be right there to get you. You have my word on that. Do you hear me?"

Shante was crying so loud that I didn't think she heard me, and then her side of the phone just went dead. That took the life out of me. I felt like somebody was holding a pillow over my face, and stopping me from breathing.

"Hello? Hello? Baby girl. Baby girl. Mikey's phone went black, and shut off.

I dropped it, and cried my heart out for the next twenty minutes. When I was strong enough to save face, I busted into the bedroom that Mikey was staying in, and found Nastia on top of him riding him with her blond head thrown back. She moaned at the top of her lungs as if he were killing her.

"Mikey! We need to talk!" I hollered.

Nastia saw that it was me, and fell off of him. "Phoenix. Oh my God, I'm so sorry. I'm sorry babe."

I waved her off. "Bitch I don't care that you fuckin him. This about my daughter. I want my baby back, Mane! I'll give you whatever you want."

He stood up, and pulled his boxers up his thighs. "Nastia give us the room for a minute. Me and the Homie need to get an understanding."

She wrapped the sheet around her body, and scooted out of the bed. Stopped in front of me. "Are you angry at me Phoenix? Can we talk about this when you're done in here?"

I took a deep breath, and looked down at her. "Bitch I'll holler at you later. I don't care who you fuck. This aint got nothin to do wit you. Its about my baby. This bitch nigga kidnapped my daughter. I want my shawty, Mane. She say mafuckas being mean to her and everythang. I don't play about my shawty."

"You did what?"" Nastia asked taking aback.

"Say Nastia this Memphis bidness. Take yo white ass out there until we figure this shit out. You getting on my nerves. You and this snitch nigga."

"White ass?" She dropped the sheet and walked up on him and grabbed him by the throat. "You son of a Bitch don't you ever talk to me like that. I'll bury your ass underneath the Statue of Liberty if I wanted too. Show me some respect." She spat.

Mikey mugged her and didn't utter a word after she released him with a push of her hand.

"You will release his daughter at once, of our deal is off. You got that?"

"But his ain't got shit to do wit you Nastia. I held up my end of shit. Now you owe me what I got coming. You're always catering to this nigga because of Taurus. Man fuck him and fuck Taurus!" He snapped.

"No fuck you! You keep my father's name out of your mouth. He's deceased. He's not here to stand up for himself but I am. So fuck you. I mean that." Natalia said, walking into the room with a scowl on her face.

Mikey smacked his lips. "Man... Now I got this bitch on my case."

Smack! Nastia hit him so hard that he spit across the blanket in the bedroom.

He grabbed her by the throat, and held her for a minute. Just as I was about to rush over to her he let her go. "Man fuck this. You know what, he can have her lil ass back. I don't need that lil girl to do what I got planned. But I'ma tell you one thing Nastia, when it comes this bidness shit, ain't no such thang in you picking sides and shit shawty. It gotta be about the money, and that nigga can't make more money for you then I can. Believe that shawty." He mugged me, and curled up his nose.

I stepped into his face. "Fuck nigga, when you gon release my baby?"

He clenched his jaw and peered into by eyes with hatred. "Soon as we get back. As soon as we get done taking care of our bidness here. Get back home to Memphis, you can have that lil brat. Like I said before it ain't about her anyway. Its about me, and you. And no matter what these bitches talking bout, before its all said and done, me and you gon handle this shit in the streets." He bumped me, and walked out of the room.

Nastia grabbed the sheets off of the floor, and covered her body, before following him. "I'll be right back." She disappeared from the room.

Natalia came and stood in front of me. "You okay Phoenix?" She rested her hand on my shoulder, and gazed into my eyes.

"I'll be better when I get my lil girl back. That fuck nigga done had my baby for way too long. Soon as I get my lil one back its gone be a problem." I usually wouldn't have made a threat out loud. That was what ignorant cowards did in order to geek themselves up, but this wasn't one of those situations. Mikey had me so angry that I found myself talking before I could stop myself. I didn't give a fuck what took place I was gon murder his ass over kidnapping my daughter, and for popping me twice. Those were two unforgivable sins.

"Damn he's bogus. What kind of man does something like that to his best friend?" She looked out of the doorway with a angry mug on her face. "Then he had the nerves to disrespect my father. That's two shots at my family at one time. He'll get his. I don't know what my mother has going on with him, but it doesn't matter. He's definitely going to get his." She kissed me on the cheek, and left the room.

80

I stood there watching the empty doorway. I had a million thoughts flowing through my mind at one time, and it made it so hard for me to focus on one thing. My head was spinning so bad that I got sick. I spent the rest of this night in my room lost in deep thought. All I kept thinking about was the fact that I was going to be getting my daughter back, and then what would happen after that. I truly felt within my soul that it was when the true war would begin, and I was going to make sure that I was ready for it.

Ghost

Chapter 10

That night, I was awakened by the squeaking of my bed springs, and from the feel of somebody's weight being added to the bed. I grabbed both Forty Fives, and sat up. Aimed them at the dark figure. "Move another inch, and on my shawty I'ma blow yo mafuckin head off of your shoulders. Now try me." The room was so dark that I couldn't see who the intruder was. Though I did smell a familiar perfume.

"Ssh, boy. Shut up and put those guns away. Its Natalia. I been thinking about you all night, and I need you to hold me. Damn." She whispered as she straddled my waist, and rested her small hands on my chest.

I slowly leaned back, lid the guns back under the pillow, and brought my hands up to her waist and held her . "Where yo mama at?

She leaned down, kissed my neck and sucked on it. "She had to step out for a minute. I think she'll be back sometime in the afternoon. Who knows, and most importantly, who cares?" Natalia's teeth nipped at my neck. "I want some of you Phoenix. I want you to fuck me. Add me to our family the way I'm supposed to be added." She slid her hands under my beater, and rubbed all over my warm skin. Her fingers traced the deep ripples of my stomach muscles. She continued to suck my neck.

I felt my temperature rising. My body began to yearn for her. I gripped her fat, soft ass. There was no panty line. I eased under her gown, and absorbed her heat, tracing a path all the way down to her pussy lips. After I ran my fingers over them, and felt her dew, I got hard as a rock.

"Cuz go down there and bless me. Put this dick in your mouth. Come on baby."

"No problem." Natalia pulled my beater over my head, and sucked all over my chest, licking the brown areolas and nipping at them with her teeth. Suddenly she was sucking further and further down. Natalia stuck her hand into my boxer hole, and pulled my piece through it. As she began stroking it up and down.

"I still can't believe how big this damn thing is. I love our family so much." She sucked the head into her mouth, and got to chopping me, slurping up and down it with reckless abandon. Natalia made sure that her mouth was full of spit as she sucked me on all fours.

I reached behind her, and gripped her ass the thin night gown up. My fingers slid down her ass crack, and ran circles around her anus. Then my finger dipped into her plump pussy. She was so hot that it felt like a silk oven. I pulled my finger out and sucked it into my mouth and tasted her salty, savory juices. Before I knew it I was fingering her again, dipping into her swimming pool.

Natalia's sucking got faster her mouth held me tighter. She licked all over the head, then would take me back in the whole way. It felt so good that I got to groaning deep within my throat, while I sucked her pussy juices off of my fingers.

"I want you to fuck me Phoenix. I want to be apart of you and our bloodline so bad." Natalia continued sucking me, d.eep throating me like a true champion.

I dipped in and out of her box and smacked her ass.

"Come on baby. Give me some of this forbidden shit. I wanna fuck you right now."

Natalia squealed, and laid on her back, opening her thick thighs wide. Her pussy opened like a rose petal. I stuck my head between her legs, sniffed that forbidden box, and licked up and down her slit before I swallowed her juices and licked it some more. I held the lips apart, and sucked in her clitoris. It was sticking out like a big nipple.

She jerked, and humped into my mouth. "Unnnn, Phoenix. It feels so good." Natalia squeezed her ripe titties, pulled on the nipples and moaned loudly.

I flicked her clit fingered her pussy hole, and ran circles with my tongue all over her love button. It got harder and harder. Natalia was so wet that it looked like she was peeing. I licked all of that shit up, and sucked hard in her clit. My fingers continued to go into overdrive. They ran in and out of her at full speed.

She humped and humped into my mouth squealing, moaning, and shaking. Her pretty feet went into the air, bent at the knees, as she came all over my face.

"Uhhh. Uhhh. Phoenix. Yes baby. Yes."

Natalia's shaking became intense as I sucked her pussy lips together, then opened them all the way up and attacked her clit again. Her ass bounced off of the bed. She pulled my face into her lap, until she came a second time.

Then I was in between her thighs. I ran that big head up and down, in between her pussy lips gathering her juices. I cocked her thighs wide open, and began to stuff my piece into her inch by inch. My dark brown dick disappeared into her small hole, opening it up wider.

She ran her tongue all over her lips.

"Yes. Put it in me. You're my family. Mine. Fuck me Phoenix. Please."

She pulled her night town all the way up, cupping her breasts. Her tongue lashed out at her hard nipples.

Her pussy was tight. Wet. Cushiony. The deeper I sunk, the better it got. The moon's light shined from outside. It casted a glow upon Natalia's pretty face. Her eyes were closed with her mouth opened wide and her juicy lips glistening. She moaned louder once I sank all the way to her bottom. I remained in place, breathing hard. I slowly kissed her sexy lips.

"You ready for me to beat this shit up?"

She slowly opened her eyes, and wrapped her thick thighs around my waist.

"Yes baby. Fuck me fa real. Show my pussy no mercy. Please, I'm your blood."

I didn't know why she loved to reiterate that portion of things, but every time she said it a tingle went through me. I pushed her knees to her chest, and leaned back, pulling my dick back as far as I could without pulling him all the way out, and then I slammed him home hard.

"Aww! " She moaned, her breathing labored.

Then I was deep stroking that pussy. Hitting that shit hard. *Bam. Bam. Bam. Bam.* Digging deeper and deeper. It was so hot and wet. The walls sucked at me. Natalia's pussy was top notch. *Stroke. Stroke. Stroke. Stroke.*

"Yes. Yes. Uh. Uh. Yes. Yes. Yes. Awwww fuck. Fuck. Ooo. Fuck me. Harder. Harder. Yes Phoenix! " She dug her nails into my back, and encouraged me to fuck her harder as she humped upward into me.

I sucked on her neck ,and continued to pound that pussy. In and out, in and out. The sloshing sound of her cat was loud in the room. The bed squeaked and the headboard tapped against the wall over and over. The noise made me go harder.

"Phoenix! Oh shit. Phoenix. Your dick. Your dick is in me. Aw fuck." Natalia's ankles beat on my shoulder blades. "Aww-oh. My family. My blood. Uhh! I'm cumming. I'm cuuummmmingg!" She screamed.

Bam. Bam. Bam. Bam. I was hitting that pussy with all of my might. That taboo shit was coming out of me. The fact that Natalia was my peoples added to the hotness of it all. She was so fuckin bad that I couldn't get over it.

"Cum in me Phoenix. Cum in me!" She pulled me down on top of her, and clung to me like a leech.

My dick continue to pound in and out of her. Just as I felt myself getting ready to cum, I pulled out and flipped her on her stomach. I pulled her up to her knees and started fucking her from the back at full speed. *Bam. Bam. Bam. Bam. Bam. Bam. Bam. Bam. Bam. Natalia's* ass jiggled along with her thighs. Her titties wobbled back and forth on her chest. I could hear them slapping against her rib cage as I pulled her hair and forced her to arch her back.

"Uh! Wait a minute Phoenix. You're. Awww-uh!" She slammed back into my lap harder and harder, swallowing my piece. Her juices ran down my dick and dripped off of my balls. I continued to plunge harder and harder. That pussy got better and better until I couldn't take the feeling no more. My body tensed up. I started to shake. My nails dug into her ass, and then I came hard. My dick was jerking and splashing Natalia's walls back to back. "Arrgh! Fuck. Fuck. Fuck. Natalia. This. That. Shit!" I groaned splashing her again and again, before falling on top of her, pumping the last bits of seed into that pussy from behind. Her ass cheeks felt hot in my lap, as I clapped and clapped them, cumming deep within her channel.

I slowly pulled out, and got between her legs again. The room had a heavy aroma of pussy and dick. She pulled me down and sucked all over my lips.

"That was awesome Phoenix. Oh my God. That was so fuckin awesome. Now I know what it feels to be apart of the family. Now we're family." She licked my lips, and sucked along my neck, holding on to me tightly.

The doors swung inward. Nastia walked into the room and flipped the lights on. She had a angry frown on her face. "What the fuck is going in here?" She snapped.

Natalia laid her head on my chest. "Get out of here mom. We're having family time right now. We'll discuss this later."

"Phoenix? What is the meaning of this?" Nastia began.

I was at a loss for words, and because I was, I didn't say shit. I grabbed a handful of Natalia's ass, and squeezed it. Shrugged my shoulders.

"Look, its room in this mafucka for you too. Ain't no sense in you getting all crazy. Its all love in this room." I continue to rub all over her daughter's ass. I even dared to play with the moist lips of her basement.

Nastia stood there for a moment, shook her head, and disappeared from the room. Before she left she closed the door back. "I should of known. Lord knows I should of known."

Natalia rubbed my chest, and kissed my lips again. "You aren't angry are you Phoenix?"

I shook my head. "Hell n'all. Your mother know what it is. I'll holler at her later. Right now let's get some zees. That pussy got me tired as hell."

"Mmm. I can get used to this." She kissed my lips again, and hugged my body tighter. In a matter of minutes we were out cold. I had the scent of her pussy on my upper lip, and that made me fall asleep with a smile on my face. Taurus's daughter had some good ass pussy.

Chapter 11

Nastia woke me up out of the bed the next morning and said it was important that she and I have a sit down. She told me to meet her in the den in twenty minutes. When Nastia saw the way her daughter was all tangled up with me, she shook her head again, before walking out of the room with it hung low.

Natalia woke up, and stretched her arms over her head. The sheet fell off of her body, exposing her perfect breasts. They wobbled on her chest. The pretty nipples were already taut. "Phoenix you better get ready for her to ream you out. She's probably going to threaten to take all her leverage away from you so that you leave me alone." Natalia sighed. "If that's the case I don't want you to worry. She's not the only connect to my father's Rebirth. Every thing that she is supplying you with, I am going to step in and double it.

Like I said before, there are things at play that you don't know about,. When the time is right, you're going to see that they are factual, and you'll never have to worry about anything else. Trust me on this." She slid her hand under the cover and took a hold of my dick, squeezing it. "I've never felt what you made me feel last night. I gotta have this close by at all times." She bent her head and put me into her mouth. Her long hair covered my entire lap.

I let her suck on my pole for five minutes, until she got it nice and hard. Then I made her straddle and slide down on me. "We got five minutes. Hurry up and make me cum in this pussy."

Natalia arched her back. "Okay daddy." She started to twerk on my dick at full speed. She held onto my shoulders, and bounced up and down. That big ass popped in my lap, time and time again. It felt like her pussy was even wetter than last night. I sucked those long nipples until they were distended from her breast. So Natalia didn't get who was in charge twisted, I held her ass, and made sure she was taking all of me. She threw her head back after a few more power strokes and began bouncing higher and higher. The headboard beat into the wall as I emptied myself inside her.

"I'm cumming. I'm cumming baby. Shit!"

Natalia popped faster, then tensed up when she felt my seed hitting her walls, and started shaking and moaning loudly, while she came all over me in rivulets.

After our fuck session, we jumped in the shower together. We washed each other's bodies from head to toe, and then I met Nastia in the den with a bottle of orange juice in my hand.

She was already seated on the couch in a blue Burberry dress. Her thighs were crossed. She had a lap top on her lap, clicking away. When I stepped into the room she looked up at me and gave me a weak smile. "Good morning Phoenix. Is that all you're having for breakfast?"

I sat on the couch, and drank half the orange juice. "What's good Nastia? What is this meeting pertaining to?" I didn't feel like getting into a big thing with her over me smashing Natalia. After all shawty was grown as hell, and she was my peoples. I was hoping she wasn't about to go off the deep end.

Nastia sat the laptop in the table in front of us. "Were you fucking her to get back at me for screwing Mikey? If so, I gotta say that was very petty. I thought we were all adults here."

"Shawty, get over yourself. I been feeling Natalia every since we were in high school, but even more so now after laying eyes on her again. That gurl is gorgeous. You know how my family get down, and you still left her alone wit me. This is your fault."

"My fault?" She touched her chest, and rolled her eyes. "So its my fault that I thought the one person on my team that I expected to protect her was her fuckin cousin? Really?"

I took another swallow of my juice. "You know what I mean. So now what? You ain't gon help me get my daughter? You finna be done fuckin wit me? Huh what?"

"Oh, none of the above. Natalia's grown. If she wants to fuck with you on that level then by all means she can do it. The reason I called you in here is so I could let you know that your little girl has been safely returned to your cousin Kamya. When you get back home she should be there. I have one more move for you and Mikey to pull off and then we'll be headed back to the States. Can you handle it?"

"Depends on what it is."

She laughed. "More of the same. There is one remaining name of my hit list that I need taken out. Once he's gone hen I can officially be the sole share holder of my father's company. With its power and leverage, I will be global. Once I am global, you will be. I mean that is if you and I still have an understanding. One romp in the sheets with Natalia surely hasn't changed your love for me now has it?"

I almost snapped my neck to look over and up at her. "Love? Man, ain't no love in none of this shit. We're all just living day by day. I had fondness, admiration and respect for you. I don't love anybody outside of my daughter." I wanted to make that perfectly clear. I'd never been in love with any female. I just didn't think my heart worked like that. I cared about Kamya, and Alicia, but I wasn't in love with them, and I damn sure wasn't in love with Nastia's ass. I loved the feel of Natalia's pussy more than I did Nastia. I'm just being honest.

Nastia was quiet for a long time. "Oh, well I didn't know that. I guess I understand it though. But anyway, that's neither here nor there. What are your intentions with Natalia? Is it just sex?" She seemed concerned. Her blue eyes pierced me.

I shrugged my shoulders. "I'm just getting to know her. I like her company. The sex is good. I feel like she's going to be my lil baby. That's all I see now."

Nastia stood up and began to pace back and forth. "Phoenix, my daughter is all that I have. She is my life. Now I'm trying my best to let the situation from last night pass, but it has to end there. There can be no more of that."

Natalia bussed through the door, with her Gucci purse draped across her shoulder. "I knew it. I just knew you would stick your nose into something that has nothin to do with you." She snapped, and came all the way into the room.

Nastia held up a hand. "Natalia, I'm going to stop you right there. You need to get the hell out of this room while I am talking to him. Get!" She pointed.

Natalia closed the door behind her, and locked it. "You want him for yourself don't you, Mom? You were so obsessed with my father. You only want to fuck with Phoenix because he looks so much like him right? Because he has the same blood! My fuckin blood!" She said through clenched teeth.

Nastia took a deep breath, and exhaled it slowly. "Natalia, you are really trying my patience right now. If you don't get the fuck out of here I will be forced to put my hands on you."

"If you were so obsessed with my father then why did you hide me from him, huh? Why did you neglect to tell him that he had a daughter who loved him? Who needed him mom, huh?" Natalia asked stepping closer to Nastia.

"I couldn't baby. My family were all racists. They would've never allowed for me to have a Black man's baby. Especially not Taurus's. There was so much had blood with him. You'll never understand what all we went through."

"So you hid me? You hid me from the fucking world. I didn't even find out that I had any Black in me until I was ten years old. When my father's execution was all over the television. Only then did you have the guts to tell me what happened. But by then it was too late. Then you hock his Rebirth off like you're the original owner. You're not mom, and what me and Phoenix have going on has nothing to do with you. He's the closest man to my father as I'm going to get. Why don't you go out and find somebody your own age?"

Nastia stepped forward, and smacked Natalia with so much venom that she fell to the floor. Her lips busted. "You disrespectful brat. You watch your mouth when you're talking to me."

I jumped up. I didn't know what to do. In my opinion this was between mother and daughter. I didn't want to get into the middle of it. But at the same time the beef sort of affected meme.

Natalia pulled a silenced nine millimeter from her purse, and aimed it at her mother. "You dirty bitch. That's the last time you're going to put your filthy hands on me. You've hated me ever since I was a baby. Regardless to how you portray me in front of other people. You're the real reason they gave my father the needle. My grandmother told me everything. She cocked the hammer.

Nastia took a step back. "Phoenix you get her and I'll make you a very rich man. Kill her and you'll never have to worry about money again."

"What?" My mind was blown. I didn't know what Natalia was talking about but the fact that Nastia was telling me to body her daughter was enough to throw me all the way off.

"You heard me. Shoot her. I know you're always packing. I'm done wit this ungrateful, disrespectful bitch."

Poof. Poof. Poof. Poof.

Nastia flew against the wall riddled by bullets. Big holes appeared in her chest. Her back slammed against it hard before she slid down it, and wound up laying on her side. Her eyes wide open. Blood rushed out of her.

Natalia stood over her with a smoking gun. "You have no idea how much this bitch has taken me through Phoenix. Looks can be deceiving. She was one of the most shiesty women you will ever run across. Some day I'll explain it to you."

I couldn't believe my eyes. It couldn't be true. There was no way that Natalia had whacked her mother in front of me. She'd killed my plug. What the fuck was I going to do now? What did this mean?"

Natalia sat down and grabbed her mother's laptop. She laid the gun beside her, and began typing away. She pulled a piece of paper out of her bra and continued to type. After a few seconds she smiled. "Got it." She leaned back the screen, and continued to type.

"Natalia, shawty, yo mama over there dead as hell and you sitting there typing away on a damn laptop. This shit ain't normal. You just killed my plug."

"I'm your plug now Phoenix. I told you I had you. Every thing that my mother was doing I'm going to be doing from here on out. The only thing is I'm going to get you all the way right." She stood up and closed the laptop. "Do you trust me?"

The puddle of blood from Nastia slid closer to my Jordans. I took a step back.

"I ain't got no other choice other than to trust you. I don't know what the fuck you got going on, but I need to make it back to Memphis by tomorrow, before that fuck nigga, Mikey even find out about this."

She came over and looked into my eyes. "Your wish is my command, daddy. From here on out I mean that. Just make your requests known and I'll make that shit happen. I have some work to do before I'm able to operate the way that I want to, but I'll get you to where you need to be tonight. I'll call the pilot, and fire up the jet."

Nastia's blood had reached the table. There was a pool of it on the carpet. Her eyes had crossed. The pupils were tiny dots. Her tongue hung out if the side of her mouth.

"Phoenix, I'm going to be getting in contact with you in a few weeks, once everything is situated here. The last person on my mother's hit list was my great uncle Ralph. He knew that my mother was going to be sending assassins at him to take his life. She was willing to do anything to take over my grand father's business, and political connections. My mom was a cut throat. My uncle Ralph is good people. He had pancreatic cancer, and he's on his way out. There are some things that I must work out with him before he kicks the bucket. I am hopeful that everything my grandfather owns will become mine. That is a bonus for you. For us. You and I will be able rebuild our family from the ground up. How does that sound to you?"

I looked over Nastia. I still couldn't believe that Natalia had wasted her. "That sounds good baby. Do your thing and I'll be ready when you call. That's my word."

She kissed my lips, and sucked on them. "I hope so baby. I'm going to definitely hold you to it. All I need is for you to trust me. Give me a few weeks, and then get ready to be a king."

***

I fucked her one last time before I jumped in the jet and made my way back to Memphis, Tennessee alone. I left Mikey's punk ass there. I had to rush back and get a hold of my daughter, Shanté. I needed to duck her off some where safe. My cartel had to get right before Mikey touched down, and I went at him full fledged. That nigga had to pay for what he'd done to my shawty. He had to pay for them slugs he'd pumped into my body too. Yeah I was bogus for fucking his wife but he'd went more than over board. I had to get his bitch ass back. That was all there was to it.

Chapter 12

As soon as the door to Kamya's house opened, Shanté rushed to me, and jumped into my arms with tears streaming down her beautiful face.

"Daddy. Daddy. I missed you so much." She cried, and wrapped her little arms tightly around my neck.

The first thing I noticed was that she smelled rank. It smelled like she'd spent most of her time in a basement, or maybe even an attic. She had on the same blue jean dress that she'd had on the last time I'd seen her.

I kissed her, and rocked her in my arms. Tears gushed out of my eyes.

"I missed you too baby. I missed you with my whole heart. Everyday I was trying to find you. I promise to never allow anything to happen to you again. Do you hear me Goddess. I'd rather die first."

"Okay daddy. Just please don't leave me again. I'm so scared without you. You have to protect me." Shante buried her face into the crux of my neck and cried a bit harder, It seemed as if she was nowhere near ready to settle down.

Kamya came and rubbed my back.

"I been hollering at him cuz. He thinks its sweet. He's supposed to be back in town in a few days. When he get back I'ma take care of him, just to show you how down for you I really am. I hate his punk ass." She whispered into my right ear canal.

Shanté slowly calmed down. "Daddy I'm so hungry. Can I have a pizza?" She said hiccuping, and crying at the same time.

I continued to bounce her up and down, patting her bottom just like I did when she was a little kid. It was the only thing that used to calm her down. "Yeah baby. I'll have Kamya order you one from Domino's. Just calm down baby. Daddy is here." I kissed her soft cheek again.

It took me a complete hour to calm my daughter down. Once she calmed down, I gave her a bath and put her into some clean clothes, fed her, and rocked her to sleep. I couldn't help dropping a few tears over the feeling of her in my arms. She felt so amazing. Shanté was the one and only true love of my life. The fact that Mikey had plans of taking her from me made me so angry that I wanted to wipe his entire bloodline off of the map. What type of man went at a nigga's eight year old daughter? Yeah he had to pay for all of this shit.

As I settled on to the couch, Kamya sat beside me. "How you holding up baby?" She laid her head on my shoulder

It was three in the morning and I was wide awake. "Man I thought I'd lost her. I can't even begin to tell you what that feels like. I still don't know where Toya is. Mikey swearing revenge for me getting Alicia pregnant, and I don't even know where me and her stand as of yet. My brain is all screwed up. I gotta get my shit together though. There are so many moves to be made. Damn life is a bitch."

Kamya raised her head, and rubbed her cheek against mine. "Phoenix you aren't alone. I hope you know that. I'm willing to ride beside you, and do whatever I can. I hate what they're taking you through. I know that some of it is self in-flicted, but at the same time I don't care. I just love you so much, and I'm ready to ride out."

What is a person in this world for if they can't ride for the people they love?" She asked, rubbing the side of my face.

I sat back on the couch, and pulled Kamya on top of me. I could feel her weight and her heat as she placed her face within the crux of my neck and inhaled my scent. My hands palmed that ass.

"I love you too, shawty. I hope you know that. I appreciate you for looking after Shanté while I was up against the ropes. I'll never forget how much you be holding me down. I mean that. Gimme some of them lips."

She pulled her head back, looked me over, and smiled. "I wanna waste that nigga for you cuz. We gotta find out how you gon let me do that. I wanna be the one to put him down. Do you understand that?"

I smiled. "Yeah boo, I hear you." I kissed her lips, and held her more firmly.

Kamya moaned, closed her eyes, and turned her head side ways as she returned my affection. Her tongue shot out of her mouth again and again. She used it to trace all over my lips. Then our digits were wrestling with one another's.

"I just love you so much Phoenix. I love you so so much. I'm ready to handle my bidness for you baby. I swear to God I am." She kissed all over my neck, and sucked on it hard, before resting her face there.

Those were the kind of words I needed to hear. In that moment I just needed a rider, a right hand. I knew that if I could trust anybody, I could trust Kamya. Our bond had always been strong. Unbreakable. I was ready to put her to test and see if she really had that killa shit in her.

***

The next morning, I ducked Kamya and Shanté off at the Four Seasons in West Memphis. I paid for the whole month, just in case it was goin take some serious grinding on my part to accomplish what I was trying to. Shanté threw a fit when it was time to leave her there with Kamya. I had to wait until she cried herself to sleep before I left. On my way back from the hotel, Smoke met up with me, along with two of his hittas. They pulled his Chevy Caprice beside my whip and he jumped out, and got in mine with two duffle bags.

"What it do, Potna? I got a hunnit bands in this bitch that belong to you. The Mound still jumping like double Dutch, and we need some more of that good Rebirth. I'd say I can handle at least twenty bricks in a week now with no effort." He unzipped one of the duffle bags, and showed me that it was filled with a bunch of ones, fives, tens, and twenties. Trap money for sure.

I nodded my head at him. "That's what's good. Now we starting to eat a lil bit. Shit finna get a whole lot better though. Mark my words. I'ma call in a order and make sure them bricks get to the Mound in a orderly fashion. You can believe that. But before we do any of that, I want you to call up your closest hittas, and I wanna use some of this cash to splurge on you niggas. This y'all day. So we gon hit up this mall and the cellphone place. I'ma pay some rents, gas bills whatever Mane, I just wanna show my love and appreciation, you feel me?"

He looked shocked. "Mane, you serious?"

"As a heart attack. Holla at cha boys, Playboy, and let's get it in."

Smoke looked over his shoulder. "You see that black van following us with the Mississippi plates, and tinted windows?"

I looked into my rear view mirror, and sure as shit stinks we were being followed. "Yeah I see it."

"Well dem my real killas. I'm talking niggas that a buck some shit down for me in a heart beat and you too because they know you be the head, and I fuck wit you the long way. All them niggas in that van starving. Struggling to make ends meet. Going through their own challenges and all that shit. If we gon splurge some cash we need to pay some bills. Get these niggas some cheap whips until we can get some classy ones. Do some grocery shopping. Mafuckas really out here starving, Mane. If you save these niggas, they gone be about that life for you."

"Den that's what we gon do, Playboy. We gon feed these niggas the way you say, and every time that money get a lil better we gon do it again. Its time to take this Cartel to the next level. Send bruh nem a text, and let's handle this bidness."

"Word, I'ma do just that." He started texting away on his phone. ''Man I already know they finna go crazy about that. Ain't nobody trying to reach for us niggas in the Mound man. Our family's out here starving. Mafuckas been hustling for five years straight and still ain't got a pot to piss in. You wanna establish some true thorough bred killas, these the fools you feed."

And that's what we did. I took the first day back from Russia, and used it to get my troops right. For the niggas in the van, I paid up all of their rents, utilities, and put five hundred dollars worth of groceries in their cribs. I gave them ten thousand dollars apiece, and had a nice long chat with each of them while we sat at the Barbecue Pit restaurant. The owner was paid a hefty amount to close the doors to his store for the four hours we needed to get an understanding. The restaurant was packed with nothing but our killers. Niggas that were born and bred in the Mound. Cats that had been there through the wars, and raids from the dirty ass law enforcement who made heir quotas by robbing us for the paper that we'd hustled for. They assaulted our men, and abused a women in more ways than one. These men were the heart and soul of the projects. I bought the Pit out, and told these killas to feast. I'd never seen niggas eat so ravenously. All I heard was smacking, laughing, and the sound of bottles being placed back on the tables after some killa downed half of it to wash down the barbecue.

Mid way through the meal, Smoke stood up with a bottle of Patron in his hand. "Say Mane, everybody listen the fuck up right now. I wanna make a toast from the heart, and I don't do this shit often, but under the circumstances I feel like I just gotta say something."

Slowly but surely the restaurant quieted to a whisper, and then it was almost silent altogether. I could still hear the sounds of utensils on plates, somebody smacking, or a mafucka burping. But for the most part Smoke had everybody's undivided attention.

"Mane, I'd like to make a toast to the big homie Phoenix for doing some shit that we ain't seen done here in the Mound. Mafuckas come up in the game and all they do is think about what's best for them, whereas the Homie done came through and made sure that all of our homes were in order first. He put a nice amount in our pockets, and pledged to keep that shit consistent. I don't know about you niggas, but I'm ready to rock my trap to the fullest, and bust my gun for this real nigga on thus Duffle Bag shit. If a mafucka cross him, they cross the whole cartel. That's just that. Now let me be the first to say that from here on out I'll go hard for you Phoenix. Morning, noon, and night. You got my loyalty, bruh. Let's take this shit to the next level. Who's with me? Stand up and pull them guns out."

"I'm wit you homie." Said a heavy set, dark skinned nigga with a bald head. He stood up and pulled out two chrome forty fives.

"Ride to the dirt nigga." Said a caramel nigga, with a bunch of muscles. He took a twelve gauge off of his lap and stood up.

"We that cartel over here boy!" Said a tall, skinny, dark skinned nigga. He upped two Glocks, and pulled a half ski mask around his face.

All around the restaurant men began to stand, brandishing their weapons. Every nigga was cocking them and pledging their loyalties to the cartel. It seemed as if everybody was strapped and ready for action. The sight was enough to make me smile and feel real confident about where I could take this unit.

Smoke held his bottle high in the air. "Say Phoenix, come on up here and say a few words, Mane. Let the fellas know what shit finna be like." He waved me to the front of the barbecue joint.

I stood up and all of the homies got to rooting for me like we was in a high school cafeteria or some shit. When I reached the front of the restaurant I held my bottle of Grey Goose in the air.

" Memphis killas. What it do baby boys?"

They began greeting me in different phrases. The entire cartel was clapping their hands together, and making all sorts of howling calls, before settling down so I could speak.

"Say Potnas, I know mafuckas been starving in the Mound for a long time, but all of that shit about to change. If you don't know who I am then you ain't from Orange Mound. Even if you do allow me to reintroduce myself. My name is Phoenix Mitchell. I was born and bred right in those project slums. No matter how much money I make or where I wind up in life, Orange Mound is my home. You know what they say, home is where the heart is. My heart bleeds the Mound fellas. I'm looking at all of you niggas and I know you fools starving. Y'all ready to get money. To eat like them suckas over in Black Haven, am I right?" I scanned the room. Every head in here was nodding including Smoke's.

"Well we finna eat more than they is. As long as you niggas keep shit one hunnit wit me I'll make sure that that broke shit stay as far away from you as China. I'm loyal to the niggas that's eating wit me. I wanna watch my niggas burp, and walk away from the table with guts as big as a pregnant woman." I paused to scan the crowd again.

"But on the contrary, if you cross me, or step outside of this family I ain't got no other choice than to wipe out whole bloodlines. I ain't playing neither. We live for each other, and we die for each other. We are our brother's keepers. Y'all got that?"

There was more nodding around the room. All eyes were trained intently on me. I liked the attention. Yeah, a nigga loved the way everybody was paying strict attention because I meant everything I said.

"With that being said, eat up, and get ready to see more money then you've ever had in your entire life. Let's eat, and show mafuckas how to look good while we doing this hustling shit. Bottles up!"

"Bottles up!" Smoke, and the rest of the crew repeated holding their drinks in the air.

"And bottoms up." I began downing my liquor, swallowing it like a fish in water. A few minutes later I stood back and watched as the rest of my crew did the same. It was time to turn all the way up.

Chapter 13

I don't know how, or where it came from, but a week later Natalia had a couple big Russians dudes pull up on me while I was coming out of the Four Seasons on a bright and sunny day in March. I was about twenty paces from my Cadillac Escalade, when the a Dominos Pizza delivery van pulled up, and slammed on its brakes in front of me. My first instincts were to jump backward, and up both of my cannons. I cocked them and aimed at the passenger's side, ready to blow his ass to Smithereens wherever that was. It was a good thing the passenger's window was rolled down.

"Wait. Wait. I have a few packages here for you courtesy of Princess Natalia." The white man with the heavy accent said.

I stepped behind one of the cars that was in the parking lot. "Man who the fuck are y'all?" I was curious. The night before Natalia and I had stayed up on the phone having a long discussion about business and how long it was taking her to get things in order. That night she'd promised me that she had a gift for me that was coming straight from somebody in our blood line. She wouldn't tell me what it was, only that I needed to do my thing with it before she met up with me in the States. Maybe this was the gift she was talking about.

"Our names don't matter." The driver said, before opening his door.

A black BMW pulled up behind the van. Both men got out of the delivery van, and got into the BMW. Before they rolled away the driver threw me the keys.

"You may want to unload it right away. The streets have too many eyes." The BMW pulled away from the parking lot.

I looked both ways, and got into the pizza delivery truck. After pulling it into a parking space, I crawled into the back of it. There were ten duffle bags on the floor in the back of it. They were stuffed and looked deformed. I pulled one closer to me, as the sun from outside beat down on my neck. Without hesitating I unzipped it, and revealed that it was packed with bricks and bricks of what I assumed to be the Rebirth. I was sure of the contents only because these bricks had the same packaging as other shipments from earlier bundles. One by one I began to unzip all of the bags to reveal the treasures inside. When I got to the last one and surmised that each bag held about twenty bricks apiece, I knew that not only was this the gift that Natalia had assured me to come, but that I was about to turn the city out.

***

I gave Smoke fifty birds and told him that after he and his Orange Mound crew popped the first forty for me, the last ten was all his. It would be that way from here on out. He went nuts. We went from having just four traps in the Mound to ten there, and fourteen in North Memphis. The objective was nothing but ten dollar hits. We sold no less, and no more. Weight was not apart of the equation. You see by popping nothing but small quantities we would be able to maximize our profits. Any hustler knows that the more weight you sell the more of a loss you wind up taking. The only benefit to moving weight was that you could get rid of the product a lot quicker. For me time wasn't really a factor. I needed the money. I had a lot of niggas eating off of my plate that depended on me to put food on their families table. Since I knew how it was, and what was expected of me, I refused to fail them. I made sure that I distributed my goods strategically, kept it potent, and accrued a nice cash flow from all sides.

Smoke and I had a trap house that was used strictly for breaking down bricks of the Rebirths and for foiling. We had another one that was used as a bang house.

After the Hypes copped our product, the feens would pay us ten dollars to come into the bang house so they could shoot their work, and mingle with the other fiends. Sometimes a feen could pay ten dollars to come in after copping a small quantity from us and they wound up using a hundred dollars worth of work just from networking on the inside. Most of them used the bang house to do their work and to fuck. I very rarely spent time inside of the house because of how bad it smelled.

If you could imagine the fragrance of dirty pussy, dick, musk, and ass, all mixed together with the smell of dope, and humidity, then you could understand why I stayed as far away from this sucker as I could. But it was a money maker. On average a minimum of a hundred addicts visited this spot a day. To be able to come inside was a thirty dollar Rebirth purchase minimum, and the ten dollar cover charge, so you can see how that quickly added up day by day. We supplied new syringes and condoms. Everything else they had to bring on their own.

Occasionally I would come through this spot with bags of Kentucky Fried Chicken, or subs, or cheese burgers. This group of addicts got to me the most. I couldn't tell you why that was, but it was the truth.

The Mound was rocking so hard, that I went from paying Links and Jack ten gees every week, to fifteen and the pay didn't even hurt my pockets because we were doing so well.

By the third week I was taking Smoke and his inner circle shopping for Sports Utility Vehicles. There was this one hype by the name of Don Summer who owned a Cadillac dealership. He told me that if I gave him a nice play on a large quantity of the Rebirth, he would plug my niggas and we could walk on the lot and buy our trucks off of it with cash money, and he would look the other way. So in the last week of the month. Me, Smoke, and eight of his homies walked onto the Escalade lot and bought ten 2020's in an array if colors. I dropped a hunnit bands and a half thang of the Rebirth. Don Summers hooked up the paper work, and we wound up rolling off of the lot one truck after the next.

I had this one nigga named, Mike from Jackson, Mississippi. He had this custom detail lot, with a crew of a hundred country boys. They specialized in illusion paint jobs, all kinds of top notch rims, interior designs, and exterior finessing. Me and the Homie Mike had gone to school together and somewhere along the way he developed a habit. That habit was his curse, but my gain. I gave him twenty gees and nine zips of the Rebirth, in exchange he flipped each one of our trucks to our own individual liking.

Me personally, my truck was black on black, but I had him put the Gucci paint job on it. He did the same thing to my leather seats on the inside. The paint was illusion. While I rolled through the streets it looked the red, blue, and gray Gucci signs were moving all over the truck. I sat it in some thirty inch gold Davins. The rims chopped no matter what took place, whether I was rolling or not. I put televisions all through that bitch, and had it banging harder than a blood from Compton. Since my shit was hitting so hard I made the tinted windows fiber glass. I even put the money green ground effects under the truck so that when we cruised at night mafuckas would know this was big money right here. I had been broke for a long time. Now that I was getting money I wanted to feel good about having it.

Smoke and his crew plushed out their whips as well. Whatever they wanted to do to their trucks I comped it. I wanted my niggas to ride how I rode. When I looked good, I wanted them to look just as good. I was eating from the buffet of life, and they would too. After we rolled from the lot, and got our shit custom detailed, Smoke announced that he was throwing a pool party at the W. later that weekend, and that he wanted me to swing through. He wanted to celebrate our newly gotten riches. Gotti and Moneybagg was supposed to be in the building. Them was my Memphis niggas. Cats from the slums that had found a way to make it out of the trenches. I was all for supporting the homeland, so I assured him I would be there.

When it came to spoiling, Shanté and Kamya, it was a whole other story. Shanté wasn't that bad. All she wanted was a bunch of technology devices. Some new top notch clothes and shoes, and to get her hair, nails and toes done. She was nine now, and was already conscious of her appearance. So I did just that. I wound up spending fifteen gees on her alone. Everything my baby wanted she got. This was my princess. The love of my life. We made a whole day of taking her wherever she wanted to go and buying her anything that she wanted. Shanté wound up falling to sleep at eight o'clock this day as opposed to her usual ten o'clock. She'd exhausted herself by hitting my pockets.

The next day, I bought Kamya a pink and black, 2020 Lexus Truck. Put the mirror tints in it, and twenty eight inch gold Pirellis. We even plushed out her insides, and hooked up her sound system. Right after leaving the car lot, we hit up Macy's so Kamya could get her Prada, Burberry, and Fendi game up to par. I couldn't see myself putting Kamya in that cheap shit so I had to get her all the way right. The smiles on her face was enough for me. She looked so good trying on the different fits and sliding her lil pretty toes into the shoes, that I got my enjoyment from simply watching her. She was bad. I got her hair, nails, toes and everything done. When she stepped out to get back into her truck that night she looked like a completely different person. Ten times colder, and I knew it wouldn't be long before I was between them thighs again.

That night we settled in and had movie night. Shanté picked some Disney movie, and we all got into the bed, and under the covers. Shanté was on one side, and Kamya was on the other. I hugged up wit my daughter while she cracked up watching her movie. I couldn't stop kissing her lil cheek, and holding her close. I loved her with all of my heart and soul. About half way through the movie I noticed Shanté was out like a light. I removed the popcorn from her hands , and set it on the night stand, kissed her forehead, and tucked her in.

Kamya picked up the loose popcorn from the bed, and tossed it into the waste basket. "She finally sleep huh?"

I rubbed Shanté's soft cheek. "Yeah, she out right now. My baby been ripping and running all day. It done finally caught up wit her." I looked over at Shanté while she slept. She looked so beautiful. The most perfect baby girl in the world.

"That's good. Come on." Kamya held out her hand for me.

I kissed Shanté again and then slid out of the bed. "What's good baby?"

"Aw nothin. I just wanna ride you on the couch in the living room. I been missing you like crazy, and for me nothing else will do. So come on." Kamya took my hand and led me into the living room. She wore a short Victoria Secrets satin night gown that stopped just under the swells of her ass cheeks. It seemed as if she'd gotten a lil thicker over the past three weeks. Her cheeks jiggled with each step that she took. The scent of her perfume trailed behind her.

When we got to the living room I took a seat on the couch, and she sat on my lap facing me. Her thick thighs were on each side. "I missed you cuz. I mean, even though I was with you for most of the day today I've still been missing you like crazy." She rested her forehead against mine and softly kissed my lips.

We kissed for two full minutes until we were both breathing hard. I cupped that ass, and began kneading that soft dough before pulling up the gown, exposing her bare flesh. Then my hands were all over her ass squeezing it. Our kissing intensified. Hungry tongues darted out for each other's mouths.

"I want some of this pussy Kamya. I wanna fuck you right now." I slid into her crack, and rubbed her pussy lips. They were dripping wet because of how much juice was oozing out of her hole. I kicked my pajama bottoms off. My dick was sticking straight up from out of my boxer hole.

She yanked her gown up, and reached between my thighs for it. Grabbed the base, and placed the head so that it poked between her lips. Her flower opened, and then I was in her hot, wet, tunnel. She held on to my shoulders, and bouncedup and down slowly at first, and then faster and faster. "Uhh! Uhh! Phoenix! I missed you. I missed you! I missed you baby!" She held her mouth wide open, bouncing. Her pussy juicing me hungrily.

I sucked all over her neck, biting along it and yanking on her hair. Kamya yelped and rode me faster. Her titties began to work their way out of her top. The spaghetti straps fell off of her shoulders. Both breasts revealed themselves. I squeezed them together, sucked on the hard nipples. I took my sweet time and licked all over them. They were so gorgeous. So perfect. It seemed like most of the females in my family were bad like this. I had yet to find some pussy in the family tree that was bunk, as weird as that sounded.

"Uhhh. Uhhhhh. Uhhhhh. Phoenix. Fuck me. Fuck. Me. Baby. Yes. Ooo. Shit!" Kamya threw her head back, and began riding me as fast as she could. Her pussy seemed to get wetter and wetter.

I held the bottom of her ass cheeks and tossed her up and down. She was sliding her along my thang and I was loving the feel of her intense swampy heat.

"I love this pussy. Shit. I love this pussy Kamya."

I pulled her to the floor and pushed her knees to her chest. My swollen manhood slid back into her box and I lost myself in the rhythm of watching myself plunging in and out of her. Her folds were doing all they could to keep me trapped, and then to push me out every time I burrowed forward. Kamya was so wet that her kitty was making smacking sounds that coupled with our moans. I splashed inside of her, and made her toot that thang in the air while I killed it from the back, with her crashing back into me harder and harder. We fell asleep curled up on the floor, with her legs wrapped around me.

She woke me up in the middle of the night to tell me that she had a plan for Mikey, and that I should just roll with it and trust her. I was so tired that I didn't think too much about it. I fell back to sleep after telling her that we would talk more about it later.

Chapter 14

The next morning I agreed to meet Alicia at a doughnut shop down the street from the Four Seasons. It was a sight to see her struggle to get her pregnant body out of her truck. Her stomach was all the way poked out. I took it upon myself to help her, even though I was trying to lean back inside of the Doughnut shop to see if anybody had followed her. After seeing her struggle, I just had to help her and my instincts to peep the scent first were thwarted.

Alicia waddled into the shop, breathing hard with one hand on her lower back. She was taking one baby step at a time. I finally helped her to get to a booth in the back of the restaurant. I'd picked one where I could still see out the big windows in the front. There was only one way into the doughnut shop and I made sure that we were sitting catty corner to its entrance, that way I could chop anything down that tried to rush in there on some bullshit. I was strapped with twin Glock Nines, both had seventeen shots apiece. I was prepared to use every last bullet if I had to.

Alicia settled across from me. Her stomach was so big at this time, she was turned sideways in her seat. She took a deep breath, and gazed over at me. I'd just put in a order for us a box of doughnuts, and a carton of milk.

"How have you been Phoenix?" She asked, pulling her hair out of her face, and tucking it behind her ear lobes.

"Better. I just got my daughter back. Before, that I was screwed up. What about yourself?"

She shrugged her shoulders. "Up and down. I wished we had a understanding as to what we're going to do when this baby comes. I mean are we going to coparent, or are we going to be together?"

113

"Be together? Whoa. Whoa. Whoa, shawty. We ain't never discussed no shit like that. I ain't no where near ready for a relationship. I got way too much shit to put in order."

A caramel sister came and placed a box of doughnuts on our table, along with the carton of whole milk. She was crazy strapped. This chick was smiling so wide you could tell that her entire mouth was full of shiny gold.

"Here y'all go shawty. Enjoy these doughnuts right here. They fresh out the oven." She looked into my eyes, and licked her lips.

"You got that Escalade looking real nice out there, lil daddy. You definitely doing yo thang." She placed her phone number on the table. "My name Candace. Call a bitch sometimes." She walked way with her ass shaking in her black, uniform pants.

Alicia looked pissed. "That bitch lucky I'm pregnant. I swear to God if I wasn't pregnant right now I would get up and fuck her up. I hate these Memphis hoes."

I grabbed a jelly doughnut and watched Candace walk behind the counter. Her ass kept my attention the whole way. As I went to put her number in my pocket, Alicia grabbed it and ripped it into shreds.

"What you doing?" I asked, then started laughing.

"Fuck her Phoenix. You need to focus on our situation at hand. Everything you saying is all about you. You're not ready for a relationship. You have a bunch of stuff that you have to take care. Phoenix what about me and this baby? What are we going to do? Mikey ain't messing wit me no more. He had some fancy lawyer draw up his annulment papers. After the separation goes through we're going to be out in the cold. Then what?"

"Never that. As long as I got breath in my body you or our child will never be out in he cold. I am more of a man thanthat.

I'm going to make sure that you have everything that you need, and then some."

"Why can't we be together Phoenix? We have a child. You know I ain't out here in these streets like that. I am a one man woman. Always have been. You were the only person that has ever been able to penetrate that bond of loyalty in me, and even then I felt like shit. You know that you and I will make a beautiful couple. Shanté already loves me."

I poured me a glass of the cold milk and sipped from it. Suddenly that good ass jelly doughnut was making my stomach turn. I wiped my mouth with a napkin.

"Alicia I got a lot of love for you but what you're asking of me right now is to do something that I know I'm not ready to do. I wouldn't do nothing but hurt you. You are looking for a man that's gone be one hunnit to you. Faithful, and all that shit. Baby, you know how much I love pussy. I'm already thinking about what Candace'll look like bent all the way over with me fucking her from the back. Now, that's bogus because we really do have our own issues to worry about right now. But you can see what I'm saying."

She scrunched her face. "You need to grow the fuck up Phoenix. You have another child on the way. A whole ass life that you're going to be responsible for. There isn't time to be chasing pussy. You have to stand up to your responsibility."

"Hold on Alicia because you're--."

"Wait, I'm not finished." She looked at the floor angrily.

"Gon head, man." I said dejectedly.

Alicia's nostrils flared. Since her pregnancy she'd gained a cute amount of weight to her face. She looked finer than I remembered. It suited her well.

"Phoenix you've ruined my marriage. You did that. You kept on coming and coming at me after knowing the feelings that I had for you. You were my weakness and you exploited it. Exploited it until you impregnated me. Now we're here. I'm pregnant and separated from my husband. I don't know which way I'm going to go with my life. All I know is that I have a baby coming soon, and my life is turned upside down. I need help, and I need you there. Why can't you be?"

"Alicia I'm not saying that I'm not going to be there. You know that I am. I may not be there in the way that you want me to be, but I will be there for you in every single way that I am supposed to be."

"I am having our child. You're supposed to be my husband if you want to be technical. I don't do this ratchet stuff. You're acting like I'm one of these gutter snipes that's coming to you about being pregnant. You and I had something special. At least that's what I thought."

I reached across the table and took a hold of her hand. "Alicia, don't start over thinking things. Look, I got you. I'ma get my things in orders and then we can revisit this whole relationship again somewhere down the road."

She snatched her hand away. "Phoenix. Ugh man. Don't give me that lame ass game you be running on these Memphis idiots. Playboy, I ain't going. You ain't finna string me along while you get what you can get out of me, when you wanna get it. N'all man. Un. Un. I am more of a Queen then that. It's either you're going to stand up and be a man right now, or you and I ain't got nothing else to say to each other. Which is it going to be?"

The door to the shop swung open, and in walked Mikey. He had two hittas behind him. He looked across the booth and spotted us and smiled. His punk ass Whispered something to his guards, and they stepped out of the shop.

My phone was out and in my lap almost immediately. I sent Smoke a quick text letting him know where I was. With who, and who had come in. I told him to book it over to Orange Mound Pastries like a-sap.

Mikey strolled over to the table, and took off his fitted cap.

"Well, well, well. Look whose here. What's y'all couldn't invite me to this lil meeting?" He looked from Alicia to me. She held her head down as if she'd been busted.

"Nigga you couldn't let me know that you was leaving Russia?"

"I don't owe you no explanations, nigga. I ain't yo bitch. Sit yo ass down and eat one of these doughnuts." I slid the box over to him.

He knocked it on the floor. "I don't want no fuckin doughnuts, nigga." He placed both of his big hands on the table. "What the fuck are y'all talking bout?"

"Mikey, you need to calm down. Phoenix and I are trying to come to an understanding about what we're going to do before and after the baby arrives. You've already made your thoughts, and plans known."

"Me?" He touched his chest and laughed.

"Bitch shut that shit up. I was the one that tried to wife yo ratchet ass. You was going behind my back and fucking my nigga. And according to the phone call, y'all was supposed to be preparing a place behind my back so y'all could do ya thing. He was gon rescue you from me, remember?" He mugged me.

"What, it ain't fun for this nigga no more now that he knows I know what it is?" He spat.

"He probably done got used to fuckin his cousin, Natalia. Or maybe Kamya. You ain't risky enough for him no more now that I know Alicia."

Alicia jerked her head back. "What is he talking about Phoenix?"

"Nigga why don't you shut that punk ass mouth before I stick something in it. Don't worry about what I'm doing."

I slid my hand around the handle of one of my Glocks. And brought it into my lap. This bitch ass nigga was striking every last one of my nerves. I finally heard what it sounded like out loud with what I was doing with Kamya and Natalia and it didn't sound too good. I mean it didn't make me feel ashamed or nothin because I knew the back stories that came along with the fuckin. But, at the same time I didn't like his chump ass putting my business out there like that.

He started laughing. "Aw, I done struck a nerve. What, I got you feeling some type of way nigga?"His bitch ass laughed some more.. "You should be."

Alicia stood up, and held her belly. "This is too much for me. What are we going to do Phoenix? Are you going to be with me or not. I need to know what my child's and my future looks like."

"Be together. Didn't you just hear what the fuck I said? And you still wanna be with this disgusting ass nigga?" Mikey snapped.

The other patrons in the restaurant turned to look at us. There were about twelve of them spread out, sitting at their tables. Candace made eye contact with me, and did the phone sign signaling for me to call her.

"This ain't got nothing to do with you Mikey. You kicked me out in the street remember? He's the one that put me up after you did that. You said you didn't want to be together any longer, yet you keep having these no good niggas following me. What is your deal?"

He took a hold of her wrist. "Bitch, you better watch your mouth, and the way you're talking to me. I'll kick that baby up out of yo ass." Mikey threatened.

I smacked his hand off of her wrist. "Bitch ass nigga get the fuck off of her. I don't know what you think this is."

He jumped up, and reached under his shirt.

"Oh yeah fuck nigga?" Dis what you want?" Before he could up his heat, he looked over and saw that I had both guns out already. The hammers cocked and ready to blow. This kept him from pulling his shit out.

"Yeah nigga. Act like you want it. I'll put three holes in yo head so fast by he time you blink you'd be dead already."

Alicia struggled to stand up.

"Y'all stop this shit. Just stop it before these people call the police. This is dumb. Mikey you and I need to talk. Phoenix we can get an understanding at another time."

Smoke came through the door with ten of my cartel savages. They all had on black shirts but the handles to their pistols could be easily seen through their shirts. Smoke walked right over to the table, and tucked his shirt behind his forty four handles.

"Fuck we got going on in here boss? I'm murdering some shit or what?" He mugged Mikey with hate in his eyes.

Mikey's boys squeezed through the door of the shop. They rushed behind him with their hands under their shirts as well. They mugged Smokes and then me.

I pulled Alicia behind me.

"Mikey what you trying to go with nigga? We can light this bitch up like a Christmas tree."

"Please y'all, don't do this. They about to call the police. Look over there." She nodded with her head toward the cashier.

It appeared that the Mexican female manager was on the phone talking hysterically. I could only imagine that she was talking to the police. She wagged her right arm as she spoke in the phone.

"Nigga I ain't bout this shit right now. Most of my Potnas got warrants. We gon definitely finish this shit at another time. Believe that." He backed away from the table.

"Alicia, bitch you're dead to me. I don't give a fuck what happen to you from here on out. Let's go fellas." They made their way out of the shop. Mikey took one glance over his shoulder before disappearing.

Smoke and our Orange Mound killas surrounded the table. "Say Phoenix, let's get the fuck out of here just in case shawty is talking to the law on that phone. Shid all of us got warrants too." He said looking past my shoulder.

I agreed, and we did just that. When we stepped outside Alicia ignored me. She got in her truck and sped away from the curb. I felt real shitty. Like I should of handled things different with her. But, I knew I wasn't ready to give her what she wanted. I was ready to be a man and take care of her and our child, but I wasn't ready to settle down, or to be tied down by one female. I was addicted to pussy, and the streets. The whole in house thing was the furthest from my mind.

Chapter 15

The next day, I found myself inside of an abandoned warehouse off of Troy Drive. Me and Smoke were meeting up with some Mexican Crew niggas that had just got in a shipment of fully automatic Tech Nines, Military edition. The plug's name was Pablo, and he and Smoke had gone to the same high school. Pablo and Smoke used to steal and sell foreign cars to the chop shops around town. So they had an ongoing relationship when it came to business.

It was four in the afternoon, when Pablo pulled up in a platinum Dodge Durango, sitting on thirty two inch Fans. He and another man jumped out of the truck, reached into the back and pulled out four big duffle bags. They carried two apiece into the warehouse and dropped them in front of Smoke, and myself.

Smoke gave Pablo a hug. "What it do Cowboy?" He patted him on the back.

Pablo, a short, slim Mexican with a mouth full of gold and diamonds, hugged him back.

"Same ol same. Moving toys like KB's you know what it is." He knelt down, unzipped one of the duffels. pulled out a Tech Nine, and handed it to Smoke.

"That shit nice and prime right there. Them politicians doing all that they can to keep the people out of America that's coming through Mexico, when me and my boys getting that good good right from the islands through Florida. They can't build a wall long enough to keep us from making millions ya feel me, Cowboy?"

"No doubt." Smoke handed me the Tech. "That's why I fuck wit you. I told my mans right here that you'd get us right, and lo and behold you have. How many you got in them bags?"

"Twenty in all. Twenty bodies, and twenty hunnit round clips. Fully automatics, with the cooling systems attached. You got something for me?"

I took off my book bag and tossed it to him. "That's fifteen gees as we discussed. Seven fifty a piece. Pardon the book bag, you know what that Trap money look like though, all dem ones and shit."

He opened the bag and pulled out a bundle of it. "This shit all spend in the end. Its good Cowboy." He gave me a half of hug. "Smoke, I take it I'ma be dealing wit him from hear on out."

Smoke shook his head. "N'all, you gon be fucking wit me, but this my boss. I'm sure by now that you've heard of the homie Phoenix. Orange Mound's head, and Don of the Duffle Bag Cartel?"

Pablo looked me up and down. "Mane, you Phoenix?

His reaction made me feel some type of way. I got on edge. My hand wavered by my waist. I was seconds away from reaching and deading this nigga. "Yeah, that's me. What's good?"

Pablo laughed. "Nigga yo name ringing all over Memphis. Every time a mafucka go to snatch up a nice amount of straps from me they always talking about they gotta be prepared for Phoenix and his savages in case y'all come Trap door kicking. Y'all got mafuckas on tremble." He cracked up. "Gotta stand clear of them Black Haven boys tho." He pulled at the hairs on his chin.

"How so?" Smoke asked.

"Yeah what you mean by that?" I added.

"Mane, I ain't know you was fucking wit Phoenix real tough, Cowboy. I just sold Dragon and his fellas a round of these bitches. If ever y'all should go to war just know that you niggas gotta go hard."

Off the back I didn't trust this Pablo stud. If it didn't take no probing to relay the information to us of what he'd just sold to Dragon and his crew, I knew that he would offer information about us to anybody he was cool with as well. That meant that he had loose lips. In the game the worst way to be demolished was if niggas had information on what you were holding.

"I would sell y'all them Mach Nineties I got in the back of the truck right now. I'm supposed to be holding them for Dragon and his Black Haven crew, but they ain't got they paper right yet. Money talks."

"How many is it?" Smoke asked, and lowering his eyes into slits.

"Its fifty of them. I want eight hunnit a piece. That's forty thousand dollars. This gone be the last shipment for a while. They trying to tighten up the border while Trump hollering this build the wall shit." He spit on the floor. "Be glad when they get his ass out of that White House.

"They out there right now?" I asked trying to visualize how things would look of I came off of that bread. I would have to move some shit around, but I could shake it."

"Yep. All fifty. Them bitches still in the boxes." He added. "Why you want 'em?"

I nodded. "Hell yeah. What you gone pop 'em for?"

"Forty gees. Just like I said."

"N'all you said you was gon pop them bitches to them Black Haven niggas for forty gees. I wanna know what you gon give them to me for now that you know that I'm rocking with Smoke."

He busted up laughing. "Man, this is bidness. Me and Smoke cool, but ain't no nigga gon come between me and my bidness. Its money over everythang. Dats just the way it is. You feel me."

Smoke stepped forward and upped his piece.

Boom. Boom. Boom.

His bullets slammed into Pablo's face, and knocked massive chunks out of it before he flopped to the floor.

I turned to Pablo's mans, and let both Glocks ride back to back. *Boom. Boom. Boom.*

He was stood up. Hole after hole entered into his body. He fell face first with his gun in his hand.

Smoke grabbed their handguns and put them on his waist. Then he snatched up two of the duffels.

"Let's ride boss. I'ma jump in they truck and meet you at the creek off of Porter Avenue. I'ma follow you. Love fool."

***

By the next morning us Orange Mound niggas were rolling around strapped to the gills, and ready to beef with anybody that wanted it. I knew that the famous saying in the game was that *you couldn't make money and beef wit niggas at the same time,* so apart of me wanted to stay clear of any unnecessary drama. But, when it came to Mikey, I knew that the drama between him and I wasn't unnecessary. It was bad blood because of Alicia. And now that I had in a sense punked him out in front of her, I knew that shit was about to get real ugly. Almost every time I rolled around in my Escalade I had two hittas in the back seats and a car following close behind ready to wet anything moving.

Smoke rolled in the passenger's seat this morning sipping on a pink Sprite. He had a Tech on his lap with a red bandana around the handle, and dark shades on his face. We'd just come from dropping off two bricks to one of the traps in the Mound. I'd noticed that there were five long lines coming from my traps in the projects. Money was flowing like clock work.

"Say Phoenix, why don't we go over there and just crush that nigga Mikey? Why are waiting around for him to do something to us first?" He asked turning up the bottle of Sprite.

I continued to roll through the city, sitting under tints. I had a Forty Five on my lap, and a gleam in my eyes. "You wanna know something?"

"What's that bruh?"

"As much as I hate that nigga Mikey, I still got a lil love for him. Me and that dat fool done been through some shit together. I know I was bogus for fucking Alicia behind his back. Had I not, we'd still be thick as thieves."

Smoke frowned. "Say Mane, fuck that nigga. He took your daughter. Popped you up and shit, and you sitting here reminiscing about the good times. Fuck his side bitch ass. Its all about the Cartel now. We're your Mikey. Scratch that, I'm your Mikey, and the Cartel is our family. Mikey always been out for his self. From what I hear he's starving his Brooklyn Fam too. Them niggas trying to find a way to become apart of our shit."

"Well that ain't happening." I bent the corner, and circled around the Mound. "This here is the home land. We die by this shit. I heard everythang that you said about Mikey, Playboy and you're right. When you're right you're right. I say its time we sweat that nigga, and then take off Dragon's head. It'll be beneficial for us to take over Black Haven. Our money will double all around the board. Everything that we are seeing now will be increased."

Smoke nodded his head. "I like the sound of that. They got crazy feens over there in Black Haven too. I'm talking the kind that live and die for this product. If we can yank that turf, man we'll be filthy rich."

"That's what we gone do. First we gone take a good look at Mikey. Get him out of the picture. Dragon is next. All of them fool's clocks are about to run out."

"Phoenix if you want, I can send a few of the homies through his spot right now. They'll go in wit guns blazing, laying shit down. I'll put out a decree that Mikey is to be bodied on sight. All you gotta do is give me the order."

I thought about that long and hard. Now every fiber of my being was ready for Mikey to be wiped off the face of the earth. I was tired of looking over my shoulder and expecting him to be there busting his gun. And I was sick of being worried about what his next move would be. He'd already got off on me more than enough. The easiest thing for me to do would have been too allow Smoke's hittas to handle my light work, but I worried about them making a mistake. I knew that Mikey was dangerous. If I exposed my hand that I was coming for him and I went about it the wrong way, he would release his goons as well. If they rode under him they had to be dirtier than a bums feet.

"N'all, I'm gone personally take that nigga's life. I owe that to my daughter, and to myself for the slugs he put inside of me. But I'll tell you what we will do. We'll--."

CRASH!

Two S.U.V.s crashed into my truck from opposite ends, boxing us in. The impact was so great that my head jerked around angrily on my neck. Then the shooting started.

Boom. Boom. Boom. Boom.

The windows to my truck shattered. I felt a hot liquid on the back of my neck and head. I grabbed my gun and busted out of the window blindly. To my right Smoke was hollering in pain.

"Pull off Phoenix. Pull off! Aww shit! He ordered.

Boom. Boom. Boom. Boom. Boom.

126

The truck rattled back and forth as I stepped on the gas and pulled away. The metal crunched, and my bumper fell off the front of my truck. More shots were fired. I raised my head to see where I was going, stepped on the gas, and slammed into a car that was coming down the side street. It spun out of control, and hit a pole.

Two of our Orange Mound vans came storming down the street. When they got in front of the trucks that had been shooting at me and Smoke they brought the vans to a halt, and slid the side doors open, before letting our fully automatic Mach's ride.

Thitta-dat. Thitta-dat. Thitta-dat. Thitta-dat. Thitta-dat. Thitta-dat.

The assaulting trucks sped away from the scene with our crew on their ass.

I witnessed all of this from my rear view mirror. Its also when I noticed that both of the niggas that was in our back seats were goners. Their heads were blown partway off of their bodies. Both were slumped in their seats. It looked crazy.

"Shoot out to my sister's crib, Mane. We need to regroup." He turned around in his seat. " Aw shit she finna be pissed Phoenix. That nigga right there is her baby daddy. He just moved here from Cali."

I jumped on the highway and headed north. I was familiar with Smoke's sister Fawna. She'd stayed in Orange Mound for most of her life. Fawna was always the good girl type. Stayed to herself, and in church. I didn't even know it was possible for her to have gotten involved with a street nigga. She was always so prim and proper.

"That was that Dragon nigga Phoenix. I know them trucks from anywhere. They had them David stars all in the paint. I told you we been beating around the bush waiting too long. Now we gotta move before mafuckas start taking the Mound for a joke." He looked into the back seat again. "Damn, they killed both of my niggas."

***

Fawna took it better then I thought. She opened the back door to my truck, with her two year old daughter on her hip, and looked inside of it. When she saw her baby father in the back slumped over with his brains hanging out of his face, she took a deep breath, and shook her head.

"How did this happen?" Fawna was five feet two inches tall, about one thirty, with natural shoulder length hair, and caramel skin.

Smoke stepped beside her. "Some niggas blind sided me and Phoenix. They see us getting money and shit and they're jealous. Don't worry we finna clap back. You know we ain't about to accept this shit lying down."

She sighed and closed the door. "He should of stayed in California. I told him to not get involved wit you." She looked over to me. "Hey Phoenix."

"What's up Fawna. Say, I'm sorry about what happened to ya mans. I got you and his shorty though for as long as I'm out here grinding you got my word on that."

She bounced her daughter up and down on her hip. "What y'all gone do wit his body?"

"That's up to you sis. I was just gone get rid of it because it'll bring so much heat, but if you wanna give him a proper funeral and all of that then that's cool, too."

She shook her head. "N'all, I ain't got no money for all of that, besides he was a dead beat anyway. It took me two months to get his ass back here from California. The whole time his daughter was suffering with reoccurring ear infections. She needed him and he wasn't there. He ain't been there for a full month in the two years that she's been alive. So n'all, he don't deserve no funeral. What y'all do with him is what y'all do wit him." She made her way into the house.

That night me and Smoke were forced to burn both of the homies in a big metal garbage can, beat their bones to dust, and dump the residue in the creek. It was what we called normalcy in the gutters of Memphis.

Ghost

Chapter 16

The following Friday night; me, Smoke, and about twenty of the homies from Orange Mound loaded up into five Chevy Astro vans, and strolled over to Black Haven. It was eleven o'clock at night, and I'd gotten word from one of the lil homies that Dragon and his potnas were having a massive celebration for four of their homies that had just come him from prison after serving bids. They'd been barbecuing, and having a project party all day and night. Smoke wanted to hit their set earlier but I was against it because I was worried about possibly hitting a bunch of innocent kids. I wasn't with that shit at all. I figured that after hours would be the best time to hit their asses up. That way we could get as many of them as possible, and it would lessen the casualties.

I sat on the floor in the middle portion of the van. I had one of the fully automatic tech nines, and a hunnit round clip slapped in that ass. There were two other hittas on the side of me. One waiting to open the door. One in the passenger's seat, and two that would throw open the back door to maximize their shooting. I was ready to go. My heart was pounding like a carpenter with a hammer in his hand.

As soon as we turned the corner into the winding road that led up to the Black Haven projects, I could hear the loud music, and people laughing, seeming to have a good old time. There was the heavy scent of barbecue, and Loud smoke in the air.

Our van creeped around the bend. It seemed like everybody was outside. I saw so many children that I immediately felt uncomfortable, but we were in too deep. I pulled the mask down over my face, and cocked my Tech.

"Awright Duffle Bag, its almost time to handle this bidness. Y'all make sure y'all try and avoid them kids,Mane. I ain't necessarily worried about the bitches, but watch them kids, Potnas. You niggas got that?"

There were head nods all around. Masks were pulled down. Fully automatics cocked. I looked behind us and saw the other vans following ours. My throat got dry.

The driver turned into the busy parking lot. It looked as if there were more than a hundred people out. Some were at their cars. Others were dancing with a partner. Music blared from more than one whip. There were woman and children everywhere. Just as I was about to call everything off, Dragon stepped out of one of the buildings with a plate of food in his hands. He strolled into the parking lot and headed toward a group of Black Haven killas that wore blue bandanas around their necks.

The van that Smoke was in sped ahead of the pack, and slammed on its brakes. The side door swung open right in front of the mass group of Black Haven residents. And then the rapid shots were fired.

Pop-pop-pop. Pop-pop-pop. Pop-pop-pop.

Our other vans came and slammed on their brakes, and more of the same took place.

Doom-doom-doom. Doom-doom-doom. Doom-doom-doom. Fire spit from their cannons.

The people ran. A bunch fell. Dragon ducked behind a car and tossed the paper plate full of food to the ground. From my vantage point I could see him up two pistols from his waist. He cocked them simultaneously.

As soon as the door to our van slid open I was chopping down his entire section. The Tech Nine hollered loudly. It shook in my hand. Beside me my shooters bucked and bucked. We were wetting every thing in sight. I sent a bunch of shots at Dragon until he rolled under a car. I didn't know of he was hit or not. I had visions of jumping out to see if he needed to be finished off when a group of niggas ran from the building bucking at our whips.

Boom. Boom. Peeyon. Peeyon.

Those were the sounds of the bullets as they coursed through the air hitting random targets. There appeared to be about twelve of them. All of them were popping.

Our troops returned fire, and immediately they began to fall one right after the other. I held my Tech and let it ride until it clicked on empty. I looked around the parking lot and saw a bunch of bodies laying on the pavement with puddles of blood underneath them.

"Let's get the fuck out of here!" I hollered.

***

That night, me and Kamya were in the bed, hugged up, while we watched the Breaking News report of what had taken place earlier that night.

"Dang Phoenix, it seem like people are just losing their mind. That is fifteen lives lost in one night. This world is coming to an end." She shook her head and continued to rub all over my abs.

"I'm thankful that you weren't over there kicking it with them Black Haven niggas. Cuz I would lose my mind if anything ever happens to you."

I held her more firmly.

"Baby, I'm good. When its my time to go its just my time. I feel like I got a long road ahead though. The last thing on my mind is meeting my Maker."

She sat up, and ran her fingers through her hair. "I got a secret date wit Mikey tomorrow. He wanna take me out somewhere. I'ma handle that nigga wherever we are. I can't focus knowing that he's alive and well. Sooner or later I know that he's going to try and do something to you. The woman in me won't and can't allow that to happen. He gotta go cuz. That's just how I feel." She climbed over my waist. Her short negligee rising on her hips.

"That nigga ain't saying where he tryna take you?"

"Nope. He just said its going to be a surprise. He told me to make sure that I didn't tell you because y'all are still experiencing bad blood."

She leaned all the way forward. The material sailed upward, and exposed her backside. There was a black thong that separated the globes. She sucked my lips. First the bottom one, then the top and ended by swiping her tongue over the both of them.

"Baby, I don't trust this nigga. What if he just trying to find another way to attack me. Say that fool snatch you up and end up holding you hostage like he did Shanté? I already gave his punk ass a mini pass over her. Well for now anyway. If something happens to you I'ma tear this mafuckin city up."

"Aw-uh." She kissed my lips again.

"You'd do all of that for me?"

Kaya's hand was between our bodies. She stroked my dick up and down, situated herself over the top of it, and then slowly worked it into her body, closing her eyes.

I felt her heat engulf me and I shuddered. It was so hot and tight.

"Hell yeah. Fuck. Yeah I'd do that for you Kamya. You're my baby. You should already know. Uh. That." I licked her neck.

"Ride me lil cuz. Ride me like a ho one time."

She bounced up and down, and popped her hips forward, over and over.

"Okay. Okay. Okay. Unnnn. Okay."

She threw her head back. Held on to my shoulders and rode me for dear life, while I rubbed all over that southern ass. That mafucka was jiggling like crazy. She was so thick down low. I couldn't get enough of that pussy.

"I'ma ride for you. Uhh. I'ma kill for you Phoenix. I swear to God I am."

Kamya popped that pussy faster and faster. Her titties were in my face. The hard nipples brushed over my lips until I trapped them, and sucked hard.

"Uhhh fuck! I love when you touch meeeee-yuh!" She rode me as fast as she could. Sap was oozing out of her pussy.

"Argh. Argh. Yeah cuz. Yeah cuz. Gimme this forbidden pussy. Gimme this shit. Uh! Uh! Hell yeah. You my bitch. Tell me you my lil bitch." I held her hips and forced her to ride me faster.

Kamya bounced up and down with her breasts smacking against her rib cage. Her tongue traced circles all around her lips.

"I'm yo bitch. I'm yours Phoenix. I'm yours. Uhh fuck!"

"I'ma kill him for you baby. That's on our blood."

She wrapped her arms around my head, and held me while she fucked my pole. Squishing sounds emanated from between our legs. Her pussy got hotter and hotter.

I stood up and held her against the wall and tossed her up and down, long stroking that fresh pussy. I felt the ridges inside of her cat. Her tunnel clung to me like a fist that was beating my meat. Kamya licked my face, and then she started sucking on my earlobe. Her tongue entered my ear canal. I couldn't help but to moan, and fuck her harder and harder.

She screamed, and dug her nails into my shoulder blades.

"You killing my pussy. You killing my pussy, Phoenix. Aww my God. I belong to you. I belong to you. I'm cumming." She was shaking like crazy. So much so, that I almost dropped her.

I fell to the floor to the floor with her and kept right on long stroking that tight, hot, pink, pussy until I came deep within her channel, shooting glob after glob. When I pulled out, I let her suck her juices from my dick. While she del throated me as best as she could I took it upon myself to lace her.

"Look, I'ma let this nigga take you out, and you gon be flirty wit him the whole time so he can try and get some of this pussy." I reached between her legs and cupped her mound. I slid my fingers up and down her silky crease that was oozing her fluids while I pinched her clit.

She popped my dick out.

"Tell me what you want me to do. Just tell me and its done."

Kamya popped me back into her mouth and proceeded to suck with reckless abandon. We made eye contact. Her light brown eyes looked so good to me.

"You gon get that nigga to get naked and away from his tool. Just when he think he about to slide in this young pussy, yo real nigga gon buss through that bitch and hit his ass up. That's gone be the end of Mikey right there."

I grabbed a handful of her hair and held onto it while her head bobbed up and down in my lap. She'd added so much spit that she made these real loud slurping sounds that sent tingles through me. I could feel her tongue tracing circles around my piece head. Kamya lightly nipped it with her teeth, and it became too much. I pulled back and came all over her lips. She opened her mouth and sucked me back in, pumping my dick up and down at full speed. I continued groaning and cringing until all of my seed was in her belly.

***

Afterwards we'd cuddled back up in the bed. She sat up and looked down at me. "You okay Phoenix?"

I'd been laying in the hotel bed thinking about Shanté. My cousin Sabrina had convinced me to allow Shanté to spend two days with her, and I'd agreed to it it. I wanted to have some alone time with Kamya anyway. We needed to get an understanding when it came down to how we were going to handle Mikey.

"Aw, I was just laying here thinking about Shanté. I was gon call over there to check on her, but seeing that it's two in the morning that don't seem too smart. I guess I'll wait for the morning."

"Phoenix, Shanté is in good hands. Dang you're over protective." She rolled her eyes.

"You should be focused on me anyway. Life is so short. We don't know how many times we'll be able to lay up like this." She snuggled up to me.

"You do know that the way you put that plan down that it may not go the way you're envisioning it. Mikey is sorta smart when he wants to be. I'm sure he expects something. I'm going to have to out think him. No matter what the end result will be the same. You'll see." She rubbed my chest.

"Do you trust me to handle my bidness?" She looked up at me and waited for my response.

"Hell yeah I do. I know you're a savage baby. I just want you to be careful. That's the most important thing to me." I kissed the side of her forehead.

"I'll murder a nigga over you quick, and wit no hesitation."

I'll do anything for you too, Phoenix. I love you with all of my heart." She hugged he and yawned.

"Can you just hold me for a few hours? I want to feel safe and secure in your arms." She climbed up further, and clung to me.

"I got you baby." I said as I felt her warmth and inhaled the natural scent of her. "Within these arms of mine you will always be safe. Kiss me before you drift off Kamya."

She raised her head and kissed my lips. Minutes later she was snoring lightly, while I rubbed all over her ass. We had to come up with an iron clad plan first thing in the morning so we could finally get rid of Mikey. Dragon would be next on my list.

Chapter 17

I wanted to go at Smoke's chin the next day, but he wound up going out of town. I was devastated. I wanted to get rid of his ass like a-sap. But it was what it was. He would be back in a few days according to a few insiders. Before he left he and Kamya got an understanding that he insisted upon. Kamya was set to go out on a date with Mikey, on the same day that Smoke threw a pool party at Coachella for majority of the Orange Mound. While everybody was popping bottles, Perks, and Oxys, pretty much enjoying themselves, I was worried sick about my lil cousin and waiting for her impending call. It was eleven o'clock at night. I stood a few feet away from the twenty five meter pool, watching a bunch of thick ass hoes jump in and out of the water wearing skimpy G strings. Their asses were so fat that I couldn't help the way my eyes were glued to them. I had a few hoes from the Mound on my list to get up with after it was all said and done.

Smoke walked up to me with a bottle of Rosé in his hand. He looked high as fuck. Knowing him, he'd probably popped a couple Perk thirties. He had a big smile on his face. His eyes were low as a basement.

"Say Mane, look at all these pretty hoes. Its pussy from wall to wall in this bitch." He took a nice swallow of the champagne again.

I looked around, the pool had to have at least a hundred bitches from the projects. Ninety percent of them were strapped. Moneybagg's '*Big Facts*' played from the speakers of the massive hotel pool area. There were a bunch of dudes there too. Most of them were from our Duffle Bag Cartel. They sat on the deck of the pool with a bottle of champagne in one hand and a blunt in the other. Some of them were singing along to the lyrics of the homie's track. About twenty feet away from the pool area we had a nice concession stand set up with all kinds of food and drinks when people got hungry. It looked real good. A few of the women from the projects ran it and kept everything in order.

"Yeah, this mafucka lit." I agreed.

There were two thick ass broads twerking against one another on the pool steps. One was a red bone, the other dark skinned and strapped. Their asses splashed the water and created a mini tidal wave. The fellas from the deck cheered them on, along with a few of the women.

Smoke leaned into my ear. "Nigga guess what?"

I continued to watch the action. Now three more females had joined the contest. They wore G strings that did little to hide their pussy lips.

"What's that?"

"We got three of the Bitches from the Mound holed up with that nigga Dragon right now. They just checked into his lil duck off in west Memphis. Lil bitches gone get shit kicked off, drop something in his drank, and then we gon trap through that bitch and finish him and a few of his potnas. Tonight gon be sweet, bruh. I'ma keep you in tune." He slapped his hand on my shoulder, and walked off.

I nodded and watched two Spanish hoes make out by the concession stand. They rubbed all over each other's asses, squeezing them, pulling their panties to the side so they could feel each other's monkeys. I was shocked at the brazen display of affection in front of everybody.

"Yo, that's what I'm talking about. Matter fact, every Bitch in here strip. I want all you hoes naked. Let's go." Smoke hollered, pulling his beater over his head. Next his thumbs were in his boxers. He pulled them down his thighs and off, revealing his piece, stroking it with his right hand.

All around everybody began to strip, niggas and bitches. The two Spanish broads by the concession stand helped each other to slide their panties down each other's ankles, and off. Once they were all naked, Smoke walked around with a glass bowl full of pills handing them out two at a time. Before he stepped away from the person he handed them to, he made sure that they popped them, then he was on to the next person. Before it was all said and done he'd made his rounds three times doping up the entire party. He walked over to me and offered me some.

"Say Boss, deze dem sixties right here. And deze is pure Mollie. You fucking around?"

I looked over the bowl as the next track by Moneybagg came out of the speakers.

"You say its a guarantee that we gon be able to move in that nigga Dragon tonight?"

He popped two of the pills and crushed them with his teeth, made a sour faces and swallowed. Behind him a small orgy appeared to be taking place.

"If not tonight, then the first thang in the morning."

"Den I'm good. I wanna turn up like a mafucka but I wanna enjoy fucking this nigga over too. So you gon head. I'ma keep my mind clear so I can finesse the plan ahead. You feel me?"

His eyes were low.

"Bruh, we from the Mound. Mafuckas been popping pills every since we were born. I'm still gon handle my bidness. I got a lot of bad blood with this clown which is why I had to set this plan in motion. I think we're getting our money right which is cool. But, we slacking on this war shit. But its all good. I'ma get all of this under control."

"What?" It sounded like he was taking a shot at my leadership.

141

Before he could answer a pretty ass dark skinned female with light brown contact lenses came and knelt in front of him. She stroked his piece, and licked it's head.

"This bitch turnt Smoke. How can a bitch be down wit that Duffle Bag shit?" She sucked him into her mouth, and started to go town. Her juicy lips pulled and tugged on him.

"Damn shawty. Wit a mouth like this I'm pretty sure we can figure something out." He closed his eyes and fucked in and out of her mouth.

Both of the Spanish broads came over and rubbed the front of my Gucci pants. The prettiest one had on a shade of red lipstick. She kissed my cheek.

"Papi, you're Phoenix right?" Her tongue trailed to my ear, then she dropped to her knees, looking up at me.

Her friend sucked on my neck. She slipped her hand past my waistband, and into my boxers before taking a hold of my dick, and squeezing it.

"Yeah, aren't you the head of the Duffle Bag Cartel?" She dropped to her knees beside her friend.

I laughed. "Yeah shawty, that's my slot. What it is?"

The one with the red lipstick worked on pulling my dick out.

"Well, word is that you're getting money. We're trying to be down by any means. Its fifteen of us. All bad, and all about our paper. What do you say we have a sit down with the two of you soon?" She looked from me to Smoke.

"Say shawty what's yo name?" I asked, as she pulled my dick out, and rubbed it along her cheek.

"Chilanga. I'm from Mexico City, baby. Loyal as they come." Her thumb traced around my dick head.

"And I'm Chili, we're sisters and looking for guidance." Her sister said, resting her cheek against Chilanga's.

The dark skinned bitch took a condom out of her bra, opened it, and placed it into her mouth. She took a hold of Smoke's piece and slid the condom down his dick, and bent over the concession stand. That fat ,chocolate booty was in the air. Below it, her cleft was shaven, and meaty.

Smoke slid into her.

"Get them bitches information, Phoenix. Its always room for hoez in our thang especially if they about them ends." He said, taking a hold of her hips and going to work, hitting that pussy hard.

Instead of letting the sisters suck me up, I pushed their heads away. My shit was still kind of tender from when me and Kamya had gotten down only a few hours prior. Plus I ain't have a condom on me, and these hoes seemed like they was bout that life. Instead I wound up getting their information, and setting up a time and place I could meet up with them. If there were fifteen bad hoes that were apart of them that looked like they looked, I knew for a fact I could turn them into profits of some kind of way. Any nigga that started out with a strip club with fifteen women was destined for greatness if he had his head on straight. I was thinking about something like that, and a whole bunch of other shit.

While I was trying to get an understanding with the Spanish women, the party turned into a straight all out orgy. Everywhere I looked a bitch was getting smashed. A nigga was getting sucked. Two hoes were eating each other's pussies. There was so much moaning and grunting going on that I couldn't think straight. After I handled my business with them I stepped out of the pool area and called Sabrina to ask her how my daughter was doing. She assured me that she was fine and sleeping. That eased my mind. We chatted for a few minutes, and then I ended our communication, and waited around for Kamya to call me with a progress report of her situation.

***

That night at around four in the morning shit kicked off with Dragon in a major way.

It was about three thirty in the morning before all the fucking began to cease at Smoke's pool party. Even though I had not indulged with any of the cuties that were on deck I was tired and worn out. Over the past few days leading up to this night I'd gotten very little sleep. I found myself either trapping like crazy, or smashing Kamya like a savage. I couldn't get enough of her forbidden box. Apparently she couldn't get enough if me either because most of the time when we were alone she was climbing on top of me, and trying to get me to slide all of my manhood inside of her kitten. She was eighteen, and as frisky as they came. On top of that she was just as obsessed with that forbidden shit as I was.

Somehow, I'd fallen asleep in the back room of the hotel where they kept a bunch of extra clean towels, when Smoke jarred me awake with a mug on his face.

"Its time big homie. That fool nice and prime. My Mound bitches say we gotta get over there right now. They say that fool leaning like a broke hip. They got his punk ass in the bed, naked and vulnerable. You ready to roll out?" He asked lifting his shirt to show me he was strapped with twin Glock Forties.

I jumped up and wiped the sleep out of my eyes. "Nigga lets go."

We rushed out of the party and jumped in my Durango and stormed over to Dragon's duck off, just as the rain began to pour from the sky. When I pulled up it was coming down full blast, with thunder and lightning and everything.

One of Smoke's lil hoes let us in through the front door. She had a sheet wrapped around her body. Shawty was a red bone with curly hair.

"Look, he in there fuckin my big sister right now. I don't care what y'all finna do but please don't hurt her. We did everything you said Smoke. Its Orange Mound til the death baby boy." She kissed him on both cheeks.

"We still get five gees a piece?"

Smoke grabbed her ass, and nodded.

"My word is one hunnit shawty. Y'all gon have that paper first thang in the morning. Let us handle this clown first. Any of his niggas been snooping around?"

"Yeah, they came through about ten minutes ago and dropped him off two duffle bags. They been strolling through every hour on the hour since we been here."

Smoke looked over at me. "How you wanna handle this shit Phoenix?"

I opened my fatigue jacket and pulled out a hunting knife that one of the fiends in the Mound had sold me for a few hits of the Rebirth. I pulled it out if the sheath.

"That nigga busted at me while I had my daughter wit me. I got something for his ass. Let's move. Shawty you get dressed." I ordered the red bone.

She nodded and jogged back into the house. Shawty s topped in the living room and dropped her sheet, and got to picking up her clothes that were discarded all over the place. There was a trail of discarded clothes that led from the living room, all the way into the back room. That is where we followed the sounds of the moaning, and bed springs going haywire.

Smoke twisted the knob on the door with his left hand, and held his gun in his right. He opened it, and a rush of sex funk wafted from the room. He slowly eased inside, opening the door far enough for me to see Dragon fuckin the shit out of the other red bone from the back.

"Uh. Uh. Shit nigga. Fuck me! Fuck me! Aw fuck yeah!" She screamed, holding onto he headboard and bouncing back into his lap. Her wide ass slapped into him loudly.

Dragon groaned, and long stroked her hard. He held on to her waist with one hand, and her right breast with another. Dogging her.

I smiled at Smoke before I went past him and took the serrated knife and slammed it into Dragon's back as hard as I could. I could feel the ridges rip through his skin before the metal hit something hard.

"Bitch ass nigga, payback is a bitch!"

He hollered out in pain and fell off of the redbone.

She screamed, before Smoke snatched her up and placed his hand around her mouth.

"Bitch shut up. Dis Orange Mound. This Project bidness. You know what it is." He assured her.

She quieted and nodded her head.

I yanked the knife out only to slam it back into his back again and again, harder and harder.

"Dats for my daughter. Dats for Sabrina, and all of deze is for me."

Over and over. The knife began to create a huge mess. Blood was every where. Dragon's head fell to his chest, lifeless. I gave his ass another ten, and then wiped the blade on the back of his neck. All I kept imagining was Shante's face when he and his crew tried to air us out and we were forced to run into some old lady's basement through the use of her cellar. Any one of his bullets could of hit my daughter. He was a true fuck nigga.

Smoke pulled me off of him.

"Aiight nigga. Aiight damn. That fool gone. He mince meat bruh. Look, its two duffels by the bed, let's see what's in them bitches."

He rushed and grabbed one and unzipped it, stuck his hand inside and came up with a bunch of ten and twenty dollar bills.

"Aw shit, what's in that one Phoenix?"

I was still breathing hard from the stabbing. The females had disappeared. I was unsure of where they were. I knelt and looked inside of the bag, and it nearly blew my mind.

Ghost

Chapter 18

"Bruh, we're talking four heads my nigga. What the fuck would Dragon be doing with four people's heads? Then the note. That mafucka said that Black Haven is ours. I'm telling you. I don't think that nigga knew what was in them bags. He was too far up them hoes asses. Somebody was sending that fool a message. We ain't the only ones coming for they neck Phoenix."

I counted the last stack of twenties that were in front of me. With it the duffle bag total had come to sixty eight thousand.

"Well they gone be hard pressed to find out that Dragon is out of the game. Its over with. I'ma send a couple vans of our hittas over there tonight to wreck that bitch. Then we gon let it calm down for a few days. Links and Jack done already told me who the law is that's patrolling the Mound. I sent them over a few packages. I'm just waiting on the reverb. Huh, this thirty gees. Your cut from that fuck nigga's demise." I pushed it across the table to him.

He grabbed his stacks, and flicked through them.

"Damn this thirty gees. Just like that?" He looked excited.

"Just like that."

I didn't really care who else was gunning for Black Haven. I had my eye on those Projects, and me and my hittas had to have them. Now that Dragon was out of the way, that was open turf. Black Haven was as good mine just like the Orange Mound when it came to the fiends.

"Man, even though this money look good, I'm telling you we gon have to go to war with somebody. I don't know who, but it definitely ain't sweet." Smoke said this, and stuffed his money in a book bag, before zipping it up.

"You say that like you're worried or something." I laughed, and tossed my money into a Gucci bag.

"Never that. I ain't never been afraid to pop them cannons, my nigga. I mean it is what it is."

He shrugged his shoulders and sat back on the couch. We were in the basement of his crib. Upstairs were his baby mother, and two daughters. Smoke was young, but he had kids spread out all over Memphis.

"Man fuck Dragon and his beefs. Its time we move through Memphis wit an iron fist. If mafuckas want it,, then they can get it. We got one more nigga to vanquish that we know of. Once we knock Mikey's head off of his shoulders then we can press forward, and really get on this money shit. If I know him like I do, he gone be coming for Black Haven as well, especially since he know ain't shit happening wit Orange Mound. That chump gon be looking to set up shop right in Black Haven."

"You think so?" Smoke asked standing up.

"I know so."

He walked to the back of his basement, and came back with an A.R.-33 assault rifle. When he got in front of me he slammed in the clip, and cocked it. Placed his eye on the scope.

"This mafucka gon shred Mikey and anybody fuckin wit that nigga. I done hated them Brooklyn clowns since day one. I can't wait to Swiss cheese they ass."

He held it against his shoulder, and continued to look through the scope. Then handed it to me.

It felt lighter then I imagined.

"This the only one we got on deck?" I asked looking that pretty muthafucka over. I gazed through the scope, and zoomed in on the far wall by tapping the trigger. It looked as if I was surveying the wall through a microscope. I knew for a fact I could set some shit off with it.

"Yeah, for now. But I got a plug on these hoes. My white homie from New Mexico fuck with them military boys over that way. He get crates of shit all the time. I put in a order for twenty of these at three hunnit a piece. When we get 'em they gon be fresh out the military crates, so its good."

"That sound like a plan to me. How many rounds the clip hold?"

I piped it out and held it in my hand. It seemed kind of short. The bullets were pointy on the ends, and copper colored.

"Thirty. But he got fifty and a hundred round clips too. The Mound finna be a fuckin problem. Memphis is ours. Its time to get them millions, Phoenix. All we gotta do is play our cards right. No matter what I'm following you until the death big bruh, you got my word on that. I'll work the side shit while you handle that up front bidness. That's how its supposed to be."

I agreed. "Man, its time to see our people eating. Ain't no more of that starving shit. I got this. I'ma put Orange Mound on my back, while I conquer the game.

"While we conquer the game big homie. Us. This here is a team sport. I'm fucking wit you the long way." He came and gave me a half of hug.

I returned his affection.

"Aiight lil homie, den let's conquer this mafucka. We gon spread the homeland all over Memphis in a major way. Mark those words. The goal is to get filthy rich, and to make mafuckas bow down by every means. We on our no mercy shit. Be ready for any and everything. Its us against the game lil bruh."

***

When I got into the hotel that night Kamya was sitting next to the window with it cracked smoking a cigarillo. She saw me walk through the door and lowered her head. She seemed defeated, and a bit sick.

I tossed the book bag on the bed, and made my way over to her. "Kamya what's the matter?" I could sense that something was seriously wrong.

She continued to hang her head. "Do you care about me Phoenix?"

"What?"

She looked up at me, and frowned. "You heard me. Do you care about me?"

I came and sat next to her. Looked her over closely. Saw the hickeys on her neck and felt angry.

"Why the fuck is you asking me that?"

She stood up.

"Don't start cursing at me and stuff because you don't know how to answer my question. Now answer the damn question. Do you care about me or not, or am I just some forbidden conquest that gives you thrills every time you fuck me!"

Kamya took two puffs of the cigarillo, and flicked it out of the window. After she walked past me she began to pace back and forth in the room. The television continued to play on the wall behind her.

I was heated right away.

"Kamya, what is wrong with you? You spend one night wit this nigga, and he got you questioning how I feel about you? Really?"

She stopped mid pace.

"Its taking you an awful long time to tell me what's good? You know what Phoenix, Mikey been your guy for a long time. He knows how you think, and some of the things that he told me blew my mind. I'm starting to question your true love for me. I swear to God I am. Let me ask you this question, am I the only cousin you doing this shit wit?"

I wasn't fuckin wit Sabrina on that level no more. Kamya was the only one who I'd for the most part cuffed. I had my mind on taking over the city. It was to the point that I couldn't even focus enough to fuck off wit Chilanga and her sister. All I thought about was the Game and Kamya, every other thought outside of those two were about Shanté. That's just what it was.

"Well?"

"Yeah Kamya, damn. What's good wit you, man?".

She placed her hand on the night table, and lowered her head.

"You lying son of a bitch. If I'm the only one that you're messing with on this level then who the fuck is Natalia?"

Damn I forgot about her. My heart dropped into my stomach. I felt sick.

"Man what the fuck y'all do, sit up and talk about me the whole time? You was supposed to be getting close to his bitch ass, so we could figure out the easiest way to go about snuffing him."

"Who the fuck is Natalia? Is she our cousin, and are you smashing this bitch too on some lovey dovey shit?!" Kamya snapped.

I closed the distance between her and myself with a couple big strides the I snatched her up, and placed her against the wall holding her by the arms.

"Baby calm yo as down. Damn. What the fuck is wrong wit you? I can't believe you're letting this nigga turn you against me."

She took a deep breath, and looked into my eyes.

"You're hurting me Phoenix. Not only are you hurting my arms right now, but you are hurting my heart." She clenched her teeth.

"Now let me go, and talk to me like a man." She paused.

"Nigga let me go!" She snapped, and tried to jerk her arm away from.

"And answer the fuckin questions."

I continued to hold her.

"I ain't on no lovey dovey shit wit nobody, but if I was it wouldn't be wit nobody but you. I love the fuck out of you Kamya. You're my baby. You already know that."

She was silent for a while. Her face seemed to soften for a few seconds. Then she frowned, and yanked her wrists away from me.

"Then who the fuck is Natalia? Ain't she our cousin? Ain't you fuckin this bitch? Don't you got feelings for her and all that?"

"Hell n'all. I just met her. I mean she cool and all, but I ain't got no feelings. You tripping." I returned. I watched her body language closely to see if there would be any changes in her.

She turned her back to me. "So are you fuckin her though?"

Since I hadn't hit Natalia's pussy since Moscow, and hadn't been in contact with her like that, and didn't know the next time that I would be I considered our fuckin to be the past, old news.

"Hell n'all I ain't fuckin her. You the only one I'm getting down wit right now. That nigga Mikey just trying to turn you against me."

Kamya sighed, and turned around to face me. She had tears streaming down her cheeks.

"Damn Phoenix. I never thought you would lie to me."

154

The bathroom door to my left swung inward. Natalia emerged from it with her long hair flowing behind her. "Phoenix? Is that really how you feel?"

I felt like all of the air had been let out of my sails. My stomach got the bubble guts. "Natalia what are you doing here?"

"Damn that Phoenix. After all I've done for you, you're going to make it seem as if I basically don't matter. Like we don't have something special? How dare you Phoenix?"

She stepped into my face. The scent of her perfume was heavy. Even in the stuck state of mind that I was in I had to admit that Natalia was fine as a muthafucka. Her piercing blue eyes were a problem for me. I couldn't stop staring into them.

"Natalia, that's my baby over there. Me and her have been through some shit. You wanted to know about the craziness that goes on inside of our family, well you're seeing it first hand. Kamya is my heart."

"It sure don't feel like Phoenix. It sucks that I had to find out about her through Mikey. I thought you and I kept it one hunnit with each other at all times. Boy, you just lied straight to my face. You are fuckin her."

Natalia picked a piece of lint off of her Fendi spring jacket.

"What are you going to do Phoenix? I mean I know that you and I have just gotten in tune with each other, but I care about you a great deal. What we have is more then just fucking." She glared at Kamya.

"You're the last piece of my father that is living on this earth, as far as I know. I'm not trying to break up anything that you two have going on. I mean I'm still figuring our family out. But I swear that I'll be everything to you that I am supposed to be, and more. I just want you to be apart of my life. I want us to get close. All of us. Even you Kamya. I'm not trying to take Phoenix away from you. Hell, I'm trying to get to know you as well. You're a very pretty female. In fact you're perfect."

Kamya mugged her.

"Look, it ain't no disrespect to you or nothin like that, but I'm still trying to figure out where you come from. Who is your mother again, and how are you related to us?"

She smiled calmly to herself.

"My mother's name was Nastia. She was Russian. My father's name was Taurus. Taurus is Phoenix's uncle."

"Taurus is her father, Phoenix? Seriously?" Kamya looked shocked.

I nodded. "Yeah, that's her pops. If you stare at her long enough you'll see some of his traits. She definitely got his dimples."

Natalia smiled. "That's what my mother used to say."

"Why do you speak about your mother in the past tense the way that you do. Isn't she still alive and well." Kamya asked.

Natalia shook her head, and looked into my eyes. "My mother passed away suddenly this year."

"I'm so sorry." Kamya offered her condolences.

"Thank you, but I'm dealing with it." She exhaled loudly, then maintained her silence. She looked from me to Kamya.

"Look, there is no reason for us to be arguing and bickering. We're all family. Kamya you are not my enemy. I don't know you, but because you are my cousin, I love you, and I want you to be apart of my life. I have been deprived of the Black side of my family for so long. I need you guys. Seriously."

Kamya nodded her head, and stepped next to me and interlocked our fingers.

"Natalia, in case y'all didn't know, this is very weird. We're family and we're standing in this room in some form of a lover's quarrel. I mean, I love Phoenix with all of my heart, but when will we go back to traditional relationships? You know what I mean."

Natalia shrugged her shoulders.

"I'm not following you. What do you mean?"

"She saying when will we start to fuck with people outside of our family?" I said, laughing.

"Oh, well I've done that my whole life. All of this is new to me but its like something in me craves it. Its weird, but then again for me its the most natural thing in the world. I'm not trying to mess with a bunch of dudes from our family. Just Phoenix. He makes me feel some type of way."

Her blue eyes were piercing mine again.

"You can do whatever you want Kamya. I want him, hungrily." She admitted.

Kamya looked her over for a long time, and yanked her hand away from mine.

"Well fuck it. You can have him. I ain't about to fight you over my cousin. Besides you got more to offer him then I do." She grabbed her bag, her jacket, and headed for the door.

I rushed over to her and grabbed her arm. "Kamya where are you going?"

She pulled her arm away aggressively.

"Don't worry about it. You can't have your cake and eat it too, Phoenix. I hope she make you real happy. I'm finna get on some normal shit. All of this is becoming too weird for me anyway. I do love you though, Phoenix."

She stepped out into the hallway, and closed the door.

I stood in front of the door going through a whole mix of emotions. I wanted to go and chase her. To bring her back to me, but something prevented it. I mean maybe she was right. Maybe things were becoming too weird. Maybe we needed to experience a taste of normalcy.

Natalia came from behind me, and slid her soft hands along my shoulders.

"Its okay Phoenix. You still got me. I'm not looking to lose you anytime soon. You mean the world to me. I just wanna see you at the top of the Game, and I wanna be responsible for putting you there." She hugged my back, and brought her hands around to my chest.

I removed her hands and faced her.

"Natalia, I don't know what you see in me, or what it is that you really want. But, before we do anything, or move forward in anyway, we need to get an understanding about this Game. I wanna be that number one nigga. I need to corner the market at every turn, and I need you to help me do that. If you wanna be my bitch, then you gon have to put in some work. I don't want nothing handed to me. I am my own man. You understand that?"

She slid out of my arms, and pulled her blouse over her head then she took a few steps and stopped to unhook her bra in the front.

"If I'm gon be your bitch, and you want all of those plugs that you speak of you're gonna have to fuck the submission into me. Starting right now. I want some of my man right now."

Chapter 19

I grabbed Natalia by the neck and slammed her in to the wall. She yelped.

"This how you wanna play shit? Huh?"

She started breathing hard.

"Ack. Ack. You heard me." Her voice was strained.

I unloosened my grip just enough to let her breathe and kissed her lips.

"I'm finna fuck this red pussy. That's what you want, ain't it bitch?"

I was choking her again, and yanking her skirt upward. My right hand went into her panties. Her pussy lips were smooth. They appeared freshly shaved. I separated them and slid my middle finger deep into her center. Her labia wrapped around it right away.

She moaned, and threw her head back and gagged. I loosened my hold.

"That's what you call a Brazilian wax Phoenix. Its nice and smooth for you. I'll always keep this twat up to par for you. I'm yours. Now fuck me into submission." She slapped me and pushed me in the chest.

Before she could get away I grabbed a handful of her hair, and yanked her backward, slung her to the floor and straddled her body.

"This what kind of games you wanna play bitch. Huh?"

"Get off of me Phoenix? Get off of me right now. I'm not playing." She swung her fists at any face.

That fight made me hard. I ripped her bra from her frame. Her breasts spilled out. I smushed her titties together, and sucked hard on first her right nipple and then her left. Pulling on them until they were rock hard. Two fingers on my right hand worked in and out of her dripping hole. Her thighs were spread wide open.

"Unn. Unn. Unn. Stop. Get the fuck off of me. Get off of me Phoenix!" Her back arched. Her mouth opened wide.

I covered it with mine.

"This my pussy Natalia. This my shit. You gon give me the key to the Game. You hear me!" I growled.

The finger fucking persisted. Faster and faster. Her lips sucked at the digits. Pussy juice dripped out of her. It saturated her yellow ass cheeks that were humping upward into my hand. Her clit was out like the tip of a pinky finger. I could smell the earthly scent of her pussy mixed with herperfume. It was alluring. The scent was enough to encourage me to go harder. The inside of her womb felt like soft, wet velvet. I pulled the fingers out and sucked them into my mouth. The flavor was salty, and pussy rich. I loved it.

"Fuck me Phoenix. Fuck me hard. Right now. Come on! Please!" Natalia begged.

I was naked in a matter of minutes. Kneeling over her and stroking my piece, while she fingered her pussy and watched me. I crawled closer and placed the head on her lips. She sucked me into her mouth, and continued to play with her gap. Pinching her clit, and running her middle finger in circles around her pearl. Her ass popped up from the ground. Juice leaked from it.

I allowed for her to deep throat me for five minutes. Just when I felt ready to cum, I pulled out, and got between her legs and positioned my dick on her hole. The lips opened right up. I slid through them with one powerful thrust.

"Awwww! Shiiiiit!" She screamed. "Yes!"

SuddenlyI was pushing her knees to her shoulders and fucking her with long strokes as hard as I could. The pussy was so wet that I was slipping in and out rapidly. A squishy sound emanated from her box. My thighs, and balls were drenched. Her scent was so heavy in the air by this point that I felt high off of her essence. I was murdering her flower.

"Uhh. Uhh. Uhh. Uhh. Fuck me Phoenix. Everything. Everything baby. Everything is yours. Aww. Shit!"

She squeezed her eyes tighter.

"Harder. Beat this pussy. Beat this pussy up."

I didn't need her to tell me what to do, I was already doing it. I was killing that shit so bad that I started to hurt myself. My dick plunged deeper and deeper. Our stomachs smacked into one another. I sucked her neck and came hard within the deepest recesses of her cat.

She must've felt it because she began to shake.

"Unnnn. Unnnn. Cum in me. Cum in meeeee Phoenix!" Natalia went into convulsions, and dragged her nails across my back.

The door swung open to the hotel room again. Kamya rushed inside of it with a gun with a silencer in her hand.

"Get up Phoenix. Get up or I swear to God I'm finna kill you and that bitch." She cocked the gun, and pulled back the hammer, ready to fire.

My dick popped out of Natalia's pussy with a loud suction sound. I jumped up with her juices dripping from the head of my dick, mixed with my own semen. I held by hands at shoulder length.

"Kamya, what the fuck is wrong wit you?"

Natalia rushed to the bed and wrapped a sheet around herself.

"This makes no sense. We aren't doing anything wrong." The edges of her long hair was matted to the side of her forehead.

Kamya pointed the gun at her.

"Bitch if you don't shut up you're going to be the first family member that I kill. You got some nerve dropping into our lives and then taking him away from me. Y'all couldn't even wait for me to get out of the building before you were fuckin. You don't give a fuck about me, Phoenix!"

While she kept the gun trained on Natalia, she said this last part screaming at me.

"Kamya, I don't know what to say. I guess, I'm sorry."

She shook her head.

"No you not Phoenix. All you care about is you. You don't care about me, or her, only yourself. It's all fun and games to you. You don't give a fuck about my feelings, or the way I feel about you. You took my fuckin virginity. You got me addicted to your ass and this is how you treat me. Its not fair. Its just not fair, Phoenix." She burst into tears.

Natalia wiggled out of the bed, and fell to the floor out of sight. I didn't know what she had up her sleeves but something wasn't right. Kamya acted as if she either didn't see her, or didn't care. Her laser focus was on me.

"Baby, put that fuckin gun down. I do care about you, and how you feel about me. Me and her getting down ain't got nothing to do with my feelings toward you. You're my heart."

I didn't know how to play this situation. I had thoughts of rushing Kamya and taking the gun way from her ass. It would have been easy. The way she was holding it a simple smack of the hand could of knocked it out of her grasp. But a major part of me didn't want to hurt her. After all it was my fault that we were in this position. I didn't have any dick control. That was my problem. I had never been able to get control of that.

"If I was your heart Phoenix you wouldn't be in here fuckin this bitch before I could even get out of the building. You don't love me. You never have. Its clear to me now. I swear I hate you right now."

Natalia grabbed a gun out of her purse, and aimed it at Kamya.

"Kamya, come on now. Drop that fuckin gun. I don't want to shoot you but I will if I have to. Please don't make me do it."

Natalia stood there naked. She tapped her trigger and a red beam appeared from her pistol. The light pinned itself on Kamya's forehead.

"Take that shit off of her head, Natalia. It ain't finna come down to that. Now I fucked up. This is my fault. Y'all cease that shit."

Kamya shook her head.

"Why should I Phoenix? Why should I cease this. You're killing me. Whether this Bitch put a bullet in my head or not, you are still killing me. I can't handle what you are doing to me. You're making me weak. I am supposed to be able to depend on you for my shelter and my strength, but I can't. You're hurting me so bad."

I'd never seen Kamya so emotional. Her state of mind was effecting me in a major way. I felt like shit. Lower then scum. I wanted to heal her in any way that I could. I honestly loved her with all of my soul. I didn't know that I meant as much to her as I really did. Now that I was conscious of her true feelings I wished that I could have handled things differently. I didn't know how for sure, but I felt that my understanding of Kamya was more clear now.

"Kamya please, baby put that gun down. This shit ain't finna go down like this."

"Listen to him, Kamya. Listen to him. Please. We're all family in this room. There is no need for blood shed. We can share him."

"Share him. Bitch!" Kamya raised the gun and aimed it at Natalia.

Natalia fired two slugs from her gun. *Boom. Boom.*

Kamya flew into the night table, and knocked the lamp off of the table. She fell to the ground and curled into a ball.

"Nooooooo!" I hollered and rushed to her side. Knelt down and picked her up. She lay weak in my arms. Two holes were in her chest. Blood gushed out of them rapidly.

"Baby. Baby. Fuck. What did you do Natalia? What did you do?" I groaned, holding her close.

Natalia got dressed.

"Phoenix. We gotta get out of here. Get her to a hospital. You known I didn't mean it. Had I now shot her she would of shot me. What would you have done?"

Kamya shook in my arms. She began to cough. Tried to utter a few words but no sound came out. Her eyes were bucked wide open.

"Phoenix. We need to get her to a hospital right away. Now! Get your ass up and get dressed."

***

I threw on my clothes as fast as I could. Then scooped Kamya, and headed down the back stairwell with her in my arms. Natalia was right behind me. When we got outside two of her body guards jumped out of her black hummer, and rushed over to us. They spoke to her in Russian. She pointed at me, said something in her foreign language, and then one of the huge men was taking Kamya from my arms and placing her inside of the hummer.

"Phoenix, come on, we'll take your truck. Let them get her to the hospital in such a way, come on we'll follow close behind.

Their hummer pulled off, and stormed out of the parking lot. They placed a siren in the window. And then I understood why Natalia preferred for them to take her.

I got behind the wheel to my truck, and started it and threw it in reverse.

"You should of never shot her Natalia. What the fuck was you thinking?"

I stepped in the gas. The truck began to move backward, but before I could get out of the parking spot, two black vans pulled in back of me and blocked my path. Fuck, they had me boxed in. The side doors to both vans swung open. I could see multiple masked gun men. Then the passenger to the first van jumped out, and the sight of Toya nearly caused me to have a heart attack. She stood back.

"Blow that muthafucka up. Kill him and that red bitch!" She ordered.

To Be Continued...
Duffle Bag Cartel 3
Coming Soon

Submission Guideline

Submit the first three chapters of your completed manuscript to ldpsubmissions@gmail.com, subject line: Your book's title. The manuscript must be in a .doc file and sent as an attachment. Document should be in Times New Roman, double spaced and in size 12 font. Also, provide your synopsis and full contact information. If sending multiple submissions, they must each be in a separate email.

Have a story but no way to send it electronically? You can still submit to LDP/Ca$h Presents. Send in the first three chapters, written or typed, of your completed manuscript to:

LDP: Submissions Dept
Po Box 870494
Mesquite, Tx 75187

DO NOT send original manuscript. Must be a duplicate.

Provide your synopsis and a cover letter containing your full contact information.

Thanks for considering LDP and Ca$h Presents.

Coming Soon from Lock Down Publications/Ca$h Presents

BOW DOWN TO MY GANGSTA

By **Ca$h**

TORN BETWEEN TWO

By **Coffee**

BLOOD STAINS OF A SHOTTA **III**

By **Jamaica**

STEADY MOBBIN **III**

By **Marcellus Allen**

BLOOD OF A BOSS **V**

By **Askari**

LOYAL TO THE GAME **IV**

LIFE OF SIN II

By **T.J. & Jelissa**

A DOPEBOY'S PRAYER **II**

By **Eddie "Wolf" Lee**

IF LOVING YOU IS WRONG… **III**

LOVE ME EVEN WHEN IT HURTS **II**

By **Jelissa**

TRUE SAVAGE **VII**

By **Chris Green**

BLAST FOR ME **III**

A BRONX TALE III

DUFFLE BAG CARTEL III

By **Ghost**

ADDICTIED TO THE DRAMA **III**

Ghost

By **Jamila Mathis**
LIPSTICK KILLAH **III**
Mimi
WHAT BAD BITCHES DO **III**
A HUSTLER'S DECEIT 3
KILL ZONE **II**
By **Aryanna**
THE COST OF LOYALTY **II**
By **Kweli**
SHE FELL IN LOVE WITH A REAL ONE **II**
By **Tamara Butler**
RENEGADE BOYS **III**
By **Meesha**
CORRUPTED BY A GANGSTA **IV**
By **Destiny Skai**
A GANGSTER'S CODE **III**
By **J-Blunt**
KING OF NEW YORK IV
RISE TO POWER III
By **T.J. Edwards**
GORILLAS IN THE BAY II
De'Kari
THE STREETS ARE CALLING II
Duquie Wilson
KINGPIN KILLAZ III
STREET KINGS 2
Hood Rich

STEADY MOBBIN' **III**

Marcellus Allen

SINS OF A HUSTLA II

ASAD

TRIGGADALE II

Elijah R. Freeman

MARRIED TO A BOSS II

By Destiny Skai & Chris Green

KINGS OF THE GAME II

Playa Ray

Available Now

RESTRAINING ORDER **I & II**

By **CA$H & Coffee**

LOVE KNOWS NO BOUNDARIES **I II & III**

By **Coffee**

RAISED AS A GOON I, II, III & IV

BRED BY THE SLUMS I, II, III

BLAST FOR ME I & II

ROTTEN TO THE CORE I III

A BRONX TALE I, II

DUFFEL BAG CARTEL I II

By **Ghost**

LAY IT DOWN **I & II**

LAST OF A DYING BREED

BLOOD STAINS OF A SHOTTA I & II

Ghost

By **Jamaica**

<u>LOYAL TO THE GAME</u>

<u>LOYAL TO THE GAME II</u>

<u>LOYAL TO THE GAME III</u>

<u>LIFE OF SIN</u>

By **TJ & Jelissa**

<u>BLOODY COMMAS I & II</u>

<u>SKI MASK CARTEL I II & III</u>

<u>KING OF NEW YORK I II,III</u>

<u>RISE TO POWER I II</u>

By **T.J. Edwards**

<u>IF LOVING HIM IS WRONG…I & II</u>

<u>LOVE ME EVEN WHEN IT HURTS</u>

By **Jelissa**

<u>WHEN THE STREETS CLAP BACK I & II III</u>

By **Jibril Williams**

<u>A DISTINGUISHED THUG STOLE MY HEART I II & III</u>

<u>LOVE SHOULDN'T HURT I II III</u>

<u>RENEGADE BOYS I & II</u>

By **Meesha**

<u>A GANGSTER'S CODE I &, II III</u>

By **J-Blunt**

<u>PUSH IT TO THE LIMIT</u>

By **Bre' Hayes**

<u>BLOOD OF A BOSS **I, II, III & IV**</u>

By **Askari**

<u>THE STREETS BLEED MURDER **I, II & III**</u>

170

THE HEART OF A GANGSTA I II& III

By **Jerry Jackson**

CUM FOR ME

CUM FOR ME 2

CUM FOR ME 3

CUM FOR ME 4

An **LDP Erotica Collaboration**

BRIDE OF A HUSTLA **I II & II**

THE FETTI GIRLS **I, II& III**

CORRUPTED BY A GANGSTA I, II & III

By **Destiny Skai**

WHEN A GOOD GIRL GOES BAD

By **Adrienne**

A GANGSTER'S REVENGE **I II III & IV**

THE BOSS MAN'S DAUGHTERS

THE BOSS MAN'S DAUGHTERS II

THE BOSSMAN'S DAUGHTERS III

THE BOSSMAN'S DAUGHTERS IV

THE BOSS MAN'S DAUGHTERS **V**

A SAVAGE LOVE **I & II**

BAE BELONGS TO ME

A HUSTLER'S DECEIT I, II, III

WHAT BAD BITCHES DO I, II

By **Aryanna**

A KINGPIN'S AMBITON

A KINGPIN'S AMBITION **II**

I MURDER FOR THE DOUGH

Ghost

By **Ambitious**

TRUE SAVAGE

TRUE SAVAGE II

TRUE SAVAGE **III**

TRUE SAVAGE **IV**

TRUE SAVAGE **V**

TRUE SAVAGE **VI**

By **Chris Green**

A DOPEBOY'S PRAYER

By **Eddie "Wolf" Lee**

THE KING CARTEL **I, II & III**

By **Frank Gresham**

THESE NIGGAS AIN'T LOYAL **I, II & III**

By **Nikki Tee**

GANGSTA SHYT **I II &III**

By **CATO**

THE ULTIMATE BETRAYAL

By **Phoenix**

BOSS'N UP **I , II & III**

By **Royal Nicole**

I LOVE YOU TO DEATH

By Destiny J

I RIDE FOR MY HITTA

I STILL RIDE FOR MY HITTA

By **Misty Holt**

LOVE & CHASIN' PAPER

By **Qay Crockett**

TO DIE IN VAIN

SINS OF A HUSTLA

By **ASAD**

BROOKLYN HUSTLAZ

By **Boogsy Morina**

BROOKLYN ON LOCK I & II

By **Sonovia**

GANGSTA CITY

By **Teddy Duke**

A DRUG KING AND HIS DIAMOND I & II III

A DOPEMAN'S RICHES

HER MAN, MINE'S TOO I, II

CASH MONEY HO'S

By Nicole Goosby

TRAPHOUSE KING **I II & III**

KINGPIN KILLAZ

STREET KINGS

By **Hood Rich**

LIPSTICK KILLAH **I, II**

CRIME OF PASSION I & II

By **Mimi**

STEADY MOBBN' **I, II**

By **Marcellus Allen**

WHO SHOT YA **I, II**

Renta

GORILLAZ IN THE BAY

DE'KARI

BOOKS BY LDP'S CEO, CA$H

TRUST IN NO MAN

TRUST IN NO MAN 2

TRUST IN NO MAN 3

BONDED BY BLOOD

SHORTY GOT A THUG

THUGS CRY

THUGS CRY 2

THUGS CRY 3

TRUST NO BITCH

TRUST NO BITCH 2

TRUST NO BITCH 3

TIL MY CASKET DROPS

RESTRAINING ORDER

RESTRAINING ORDER 2

IN LOVE WITH A CONVICT

Coming Soon

BONDED BY BLOOD 2

BOW DOWN TO MY GANGSTA

Ghost

CPSIA information can be obtained
at www.ICGtesting.com
Printed in the USA
BVHW040558260521
608172BV00012B/183